Responsible Journalism

Responsible Journalism

A Practical Guide for Working and Aspiring Journalists

Jeff Alan

Foreword by Hugh Downs

Bonus Books, Inc.
Chicago, Illinois

05   04   03   02   01   5   4   3   2   1

Library of Congress Control Number: 2001093441
ISBN: 1-56625-168-0

Bonus Books, Inc.
160 East Illinois Street
Chicago, IL 60611

Printed in the United States of America

To my father

Table of Contents

Foreword

by Hugh Downs

A journalist can wear one or all of three hats—which are very different. The first hat is reportage. Reportage, when done responsibly, is simply reporting truthfully an event or situation, and keeping it in reasonable perspective. A favorite historical example of the failure to do this is the sensational account in 1910 newspapers of the appearance of Halley's comet—a much more dramatic event than the 1986 appearance. It was reported that the earth would pass through the tail of the comet, and that that tail was made up of poisonous gases. This caused enormous anguish to a percentage of the public. If the story had been told completely and in perspective, no one would have panicked. In the vacuum of space, the gases of the tail of Halley's comet are so tenuous—so thin and spread out over millions of miles—that if the whole tail were compressed into a solid, you could put it in a briefcase handily. There were no instruments then (nor are there now) that could measure the amount of "poisonous gases" that would be added to the earth's atmosphere. Minuscule! But that's not the way the papers reported it.

In addition to reportage, there is commentary—editorials that try to persuade. This is legitimate journalism as long as it is labeled as what it is. Editorials should not be subtly inserted into news stories.

The third aspect of responsible journalism has to do with the integrity of a journalist in protecting sources and keeping promises. One relatively recent example of what I think was stout integrity is when Walter Cronkite was vacationing on Martha's Vineyard in his yacht, at the time the Clinton family was really bedeviled with the Monica Lewinsky story. Copy on the subject was so hot that much money changed hands for the tiniest tidbit. Cronkite offered Clinton

and Hillary and Chelsea sanctuary aboard his yacht, and they accepted. For a whole day they escaped the paparazzi, and had a good time
on the water. When they left at the end of the day, the press closed in
on Cronkite and really pressed him with huge offers, hoping he would
give them information on anything the family had said or done, or
their attitude, mood—anything. Cronkite said nothing. He had promised the Clintons sanctuary, and that's what they got. To my mind,
this is why Cronkite is still voted the most trusted man in America.

On protection of sources, I think if you accept someone as a
source, responsible journalism entails not divulging the source even if
you find yourself in contempt of court. There are instances, however, when I would not accept such a source. If a serial killer contacted
me and said he would give me a story, or sought my help in making a
deal with authorities but wanted my promise that I would not leak his
whereabouts, I would have to turn him down. I'd tell him that if
I found out where he was I would have to turn him in, because if I
knew that protecting him as a source could mean further murders, my
responsibility would be to the public and not to him as a source.

This useful volume not only articulates these and other ideas
on journalistic responsibility, but outlines with clarity the techniques
for identifying the principles involved and staying on the track. And
it points out the happy fact that doing responsible journalism is ultimately the most expedient path the career journalist can follow.

As a handbook, it should prove useful for a long time.

HUGH DOWNS

Acknowledgments

Wh

en you step up to the microphone to accept an award, you don't want to forget anyone who contributed to your achievement. I called upon many of my fellow journalists for help with this work. Many of them I have known for years. Some worked with me in the past; some work with me today. Others I had the honor of meeting for the first time.

By my best calculation, I have now spent more than 50,000 hours of my life in a newsroom. Just when I think I have seen everything, something new and different happens. I thank my first news director, Jack London, for setting me off on the right road. For the good times and the not so good times, I thank everyone I have worked with. The learning experience has been invaluable.

I could not have written this book without the foresight of the editors at Bonus Books, who knew how important this book would be to both working and aspiring journalists.

To my graphic designer and first proofreader, the person who shares my name (and everything else), Susan Alan. To Devon Freeny, my editor, who guided me through this entire process. A very special thanks to Hugh Downs for his eloquent foreword.

I called upon some extraordinary minds to contribute to this book. Dr. Ann Utterback wrote a fascinating section on how the tone of your voice can get you in trouble. Mike Freedman of George Washington University composed a piece on radio broadcasting. Michelle Betz gathered the faculty of Central Florida University and came up with the responsibility test. Frank Sennett contributed a section on the newspaper correction process. Bill Dedman will put your research skills to the test. Dana Adams gives valuable makeup advice, and noted media attorney Richard Goehler presents his pre-broadcast review process.

You'll recognize the names of many of the other extraordinary writers and reporters who made contributions. There are stories and advice from television journalists Sam Donaldson, Page Hopkins, Donya Archer, Patrick Emory, Paul Brown, Jean Jackson, Laurie Stein and Mindy Basara; from news directors Jeff Wald, Dan Bradley, Lynn Heider, Alan Little, Peter Nuemann and Jonathan Knopf; and from many others.

Thanks also to all the television stations and networks, and others who supplied pictures for this book.

Introduction

Ambassador Hotel, Los Angeles
June 5, 1968   12:13 a.m.

I was young and inexperienced, standing on the podium just a few
feet from Robert Kennedy. He held up his hand and flashed the victory sign, having just won the California presidential primary. As he
walked toward me, little did I know that what was about to happen
would dedicate me to journalism and change my life.

I had toured with Robert Kennedy for the last two weeks of
his California campaign. I was just out of high school and reporting
for two Los Angeles radio stations that night. You could see that

Courtesy California Archives

Kennedy was tired but thrilled. He proclaimed, "It's on to Chicago and let's win there." He stepped back from the lectern and turned away from me to exit through the crowd. In a split-second decision, Kennedy's aides turned him around to exit through a hallway door leading to the kitchen of the Ambassador Hotel. As he moved past me, I followed.

I was a few steps behind the senator when I heard a series of loud popping noises. Something was very wrong. Kennedy fell backward toward me; there was chaos as the guards shouted, "Get back." The senator was on the ground; I saw blood and then was forcibly pushed out of the room. It all happened very fast. People were yelling and disoriented. With my tape recorder running, I began to report:

Kennedy has been shot—they think Kennedy has been shot. Robert Kennedy has been shot in this room off to the side of the hall. I was near the senator; we heard what appeared to be gun shots from inside this room. It's mass chaos. You heard it as it happened.

[Ethel Kennedy screams, "Let a doctor get to him."] We don't know what has happened; it's mass chaos. Someone else has been shot. I see another person who was next to Kennedy who was shot in the forehead, and she is bleeding badly. Yet another person was shot near Kennedy. It was mass chaos here; we did hear gunshots from the hallway and there are people running everywhere.

I was not sure what I had seen. I had no way to feed my tape and had to report what I knew, which was not much. My emotions got in the way; my reporting was fragmented and disjointed. I was back in the ballroom. With people emerging from the kitchen behind me doused in blood, I assumed they had all been shot. Actually, they had been cut by broken champagne glasses. I also assumed Kennedy had been shot. I ran to the reporters' phone bank, grabbed one phone and pushed a woman away from a second. With a phone in each hand I went on the air live on two stations at once. I did not know that I was the first to report that Kennedy had been shot.

Although I was reasonably sure what I witnessed, at that point it was all assumption, not fact. A campaign worker shouted over the PA, "Is there a doctor in the room?" People were still emerging from the kitchen bleeding, dazed and in shock. I continued to piece together

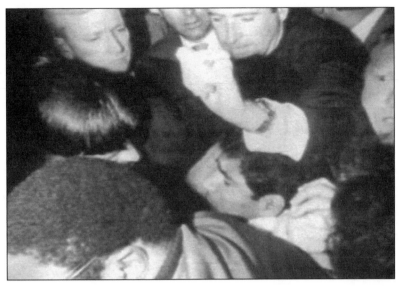

Courtesy California Archives

what I had just seen, assuming that I had all the facts without weighing all the evidence. Even though it turned out that Kennedy had indeed been hit, I had no way of knowing at the time. My overzealous reporting could have been inaccurate and irresponsible.

I learned many lessons that night as I embarked on my career in journalism. And over the course of my career, I have learned many more. In this book, I will share these lessons, as well as the thoughts of my fellow journalists, on the topic of responsible journalism.

In today's journalistic climate, much is getting lost, too many people are taking too many liberties and the level of personal responsibility is being diminished. We write and rewrite history every single day. Sometimes we become part of history ourselves. It's our words and pictures that will become the window into this moment in time. These indelible marks must be left responsibly.

CHAPTER 1

What Is Responsible Journalism?

I have an old-fashioned belief that Americans like to make up their own minds on the basis of all available information. The conclusions you draw are your own affair. I have no desire to influence them, and shall leave such efforts to those who have more confidence in their own judgment than I have in mine.

Edward R. Murrow

When you board a commercial airliner, you are comforted to know that a system of checks and balances is in place to assure a safe flight. The pilots go through an extensive checklist before the plane pushes back from the gate. Passengers expect these measures to be taken for their protection.

Think of yourself as a commercial pilot and your readers, listeners or viewers as the passengers. What type of safety precautions do you take to ensure the well-being of the viewing public? Haste caused by competition or deadlines is like a pilot running onto the plane at the last moment, forgetting about the checklist and taking off. It would be unsettling to be a passenger on that plane.

When a person reads the daily newspaper, turns on the radio or sits down to watch the six o'clock news, he or she expects to be responsibly informed.

To help you meet these expectations of quality, two organizations have created their own "safety checklists." Both the Radio-Television News Directors Association and the Society of Professional Journalists have set down ethical guidelines for responsible journalism.

The major points of the RTNDA code of ethics are:

- Public Trust
- Truth
- Fairness
- Integrity
- Independence
- Accountability

The Society of Professional Journalists' main points are:

- Seek Truth and Report It
- Minimize Harm
- Act Independently
- Be Accountable

The full text of these guidelines can be found in Appendix C.

Does the Public Trust the Media?

These guidelines are the ideal, but all too often the reality of journalism today falls short. As part of the Fair Press Project, the Freedom Forum surveyed members of the public and asked what bothers them about the news media.

Respondents spoke compellingly of their experiences with broadcast and print journalism and their observations about the behavior of journalists. They affirmed their belief in the press as an important institution in our democracy, but were unsparing in expressing concerns about basic journalistic practices they regard as unfair:

- News gets too much too wrong too often; it is not factually accurate often enough.
- National networks, local news stations and newspapers are unwilling to correct mistakes fully, candidly, prominently, promptly and gracefully.
- The press is biased—not with a liberal slant but with a negative one. There is too much focus on what is wrong and what is in conflict, and not enough emphasis on what is working and succeeding. There is too much focus on the failures of the system and not enough on the victories of life and the people who live in our communities.

- Journalists are seen as arrogant and elitist. Too often they convey an attitude that "we are better than you."
- Journalists are too inclined to jump to conclusions about where truth lies and are unwilling to challenge their initial take on stories.
- Broadcast and newspaper journalism does not reflect the entire community fully and fairly. Specifically, the public is concerned that progress in coverage of minority communities is leveling off, and—because there are not enough journalists of color on staff or in leadership positions—stories are not sufficiently attuned to cultural differences and nuances in an increasingly diverse society.
- The public respects the professional and technical skills journalists bring to their craft, but fears that journalists don't know enough. Specifically, they don't have an authoritative understanding of the complicated world they have to explain to the public.

Basic Rules

Regaining the trust of the public is not an easy task. A journalist must consider many different factors if he or she wants to be responsible, and many of them will be examined in depth in the following chapters. But, to begin, here are six general rules to help guide you in your everyday reporting.

Rule One: Listen and Evaluate

It was 1968; the war in Vietnam was going badly for the United States. There were protests in one city or another almost every day. I was interviewing Barry Goldwater, then a senator. I asked, "Senator Goldwater, last night on the Mayor Yorty Show [the Mayor of Los Angeles had his own talk show] you said we should bomb the city of Hiphong and at the same time you said you agreed with President Johnson's current policy against those type of bombings. Would you comment on that?" Goldwater looked me squarely in the eye and replied, "No, no, young man, I said we should bomb the *docks* of Hiphong, and as far as agreeing with President Johnson, yes, I condone his policy."

From "An Hour With Barry Goldwater"

I returned to my newsroom proud to have gotten a quote on the story of the day. My news director's door flew open and he yelled, "Jeff, get in here" (not quite in that language). Terrified, I walked in. He showed me the Goldwater bite and asked me what was wrong with it. I didn't know. He loudly explained that the city and docks of Hiphong are the same thing and agreeing and condoning are also the same. What Goldwater did was turn my question around in his answer and still contradicted himself. I admit, I didn't catch it.

From that moment on I was careful to listen to every answer, especially from politicians, to see if the person was actually answering my question with an answer I could use on the air.

A week later Ronald Reagan, then the governor of California, did the very same thing to me. When I confronted him by saying, "Governor, you didn't answer my question," he reacted angrily and walked away. That reaction made the air on all three network affiliates in Los Angeles.

Years later, while doing the one-hour special "An Interview with Barry Goldwater," I asked the Senator if he remembered the tactic of answering a question about contradiction with a contradictory answer and he responded, "It happens all the time. It's a style that's used by many politicians to skirt those type of questions. As a matter of fact, I taught Reagan how to do that."

I learned many valuable lessons in my first few years in this business. Listening and evaluating whether I had a usable answer was one of the biggest. We tend to start thinking of the next question to ask while the person we are interviewing is responding to the current one. Take the extra minute or two to jot down your most important questions in advance. Then, while you're listening, be thinking about rebuttal or follow-up questions instead.

If you don't get a direct answer to your question, the responsible thing to do is to is to ask for a direct answer or a "no comment." There's a famous quote from Paul Fussell:

"What someone doesn't want you to publish is journalism; all else is publicity."

Sometimes what's *not* said can be as captivating as what is. On television some of the most memorable moments come when the subject of a story doesn't know what to say or refuses to comment. A facial expression can often tell the story all by itself.

The interview is the single most important part of any news story. It's how we gather information. How you conduct your interview will make or break your story. Common sense? Sure, but I'm surprised at how many reporters do a poor to adequate job at interviewing. Listening can go a long way. Don't jump into someone's answer with another question; let him or her finish.

Rule Two: The Silence Rule

When interviewing, the silent pause is your friend. When you are interviewing someone and he or she stops talking, don't blurt out the next question. See what your subject says next.

You may find that the very next thing he or she says is the best part of your interview.

When Ronald Reagan was governor of California, Drew Pearson, a Washington columnist, wrote an article in which he called the governor a homosexual. The media gathered at a private airport and greeted Reagan with cameras and microphones as he stepped off the plane. "What's your response to being called a homosexual?" I asked. "Come on," he said, "that's absurd. I'm not going to comment on anything that ridiculous."

There was silence. No one started to ask another question. Suddenly, not knowing what else to say, Reagan blurted out, "Mr. Pearson is just trying to start something, because he's the homosexual, not me.

Ask him." It was the accusatory quote from Reagan that everyone used that night on the news and that showed up as headlines in the morning papers.

Another good example is when I asked Barry Goldwater about unnecessary wars the United States was involved in or a party to. He talked about Vietnam and then there was a pause. I said nothing and waited. Goldwater then proclaimed, "We didn't have to go to war with Mexico, but we did. Most of the land in California, Arizona and New Mexico we got from Mexico in a war we didn't need to fight. So they understandably are upset with us and they'll tell me over a few tequilas that someday they are going to get it back. I don't want Mexico feeling so strong that they can force the United States into decisions."

As Mark Twain once said:

"It's better to keep your mouth shut and appear stupid than to open it and remove all doubt."

Rule Three: Stop and Look Around

If you don't learn anything else in your career, learn this: there is always a story behind the story! A photographer for KSTP-TV in Minneapolis was at the airport on an assigned story when he looked out the window and saw something shocking.

News footage shot by KSTP showed three Northwest Airlines baggage handlers taking packages off a plane at Minneapolis–St. Paul International Airport, and tossing them over their heads, behind their backs, high into the air and into a bin. The videotape also showed one of the packages crashing to the ground.

"We were embarrassed and disturbed by their actions," said Northwest vice president Dirk McMahon.

The footage ended up on all three network newscasts and was played repeatedly on the cable news channels. The Northwest employees were suspended for their outrageous behavior. All this because a local news crew was on top of its game that day.

You never know when a story is staring you right in the face. A questionable billboard as you're driving down the road; a group of people clearly where they would not normally be; picketers where there was no known labor problem; or packs of stray dogs roaming the streets. Human-interest stories are all around you.

Journalistic enterprise is what will set you apart from the other reporters in your newsroom. If you're the reporter, anchor, producer

Courtesy KSTP-TV

or editor who contributes to the daily editorial meetings with a good idea, you'll be a hero.

Over the years my producers have said, "You know, I was out at a restaurant last night and I heard people talking about…" This starts a conversation in the news meeting and, before you know it, we have a story. For example, a producer once said, "I heard people saying they won't come downtown on the weekends because they always get parking tickets. They can't even eat dinner or go shopping because they'd have to run out to the meter every hour." In a city that was trying to revitalize its downtown, this seemed counterproductive. The station did a story on the subject, and the next thing you know the city stopped giving out parking tickets on the weekends.

Another good example from the world of print journalism: There was an accident and a local newspaper reporter went to the hospital for a follow-up on the injured. While he was there he overheard a woman yelling at an admitting nurse, "Why did the ambulance bring my husband here? There are two other hospitals closer to my house. It wasted ten minutes, and if anything happens to him I'm getting a lawyer." The reporter told his city editor, who told him to look into the situation. The reporter found out that certain ambulance companies have deals with certain hospitals to bring the sick and injured to them instead of other hospitals. The story ran as a front-page item; there was an investigation and the hospitals' policies were changed.

When a story creates a new policy that benefits the public good, it is responsible journalism.

Rule Four: Be Sensitive

One could argue that reporters should not interview victims, survivors and emotionally distressed people, but it's part of our job. Following the crash of U.S. Airways Flight 427 near Pittsburgh, we quickly realized that 14 of the crash victims resided in our market. This was a tragedy, and the last person grieving families wanted to see was a reporter. We had to be very sensitive to the pain this horrible event had caused, and made contact indirectly through relatives, friends or colleagues. We asked if the family wanted a video tribute to the loved one(s) lost in the crash. We assured them that this would be done in accordance with any rules they wished to impose. Surprisingly, all but a few of the families said yes. Some wanted us to wait until after the funeral and others wanted to talk right away. My reporters were coached on how to be respectful and compassionate at all times while in the presence of the family.

Tragedy is a fact of life for journalists. Following the Columbine shootings in Colorado, journalists from around the globe descended on that city. Many handled themselves in a sensitive and professional manner; others did not.

A freelance photographer named William Hart was working for the *Greeley Tribune*. He was taking pictures at the memorial banner that was signed by grieving students and teachers.

One television anchor from the Midwest was having trouble getting interviews. He stuck his arm through the center of the banner and put a microphone right in front of a young girl who was in tears as she laid flowers on the ground. This is behavior unbecoming a professional journalist.

William Hart wrote of the incident, "The girl was very upset and let them know this. I was actually upset myself."

Remember these points when approaching a person who is grieving:

Courtesy William Hart

- As a manager, always send a reporter who can be compassionate and sensitive to the issues involved.
- As a reporter, be a good listener. Show concern by using phases like, "I can't imagine what you are going though right now." Think about what you are going to say and ask before you arrive at the story.
- As a photographer, stay behind at first and let the reporter indicate when it's best to have a camera present.

Rule Five: Don't be Impulsive—Competition Can Cloud Your Judgment

Many reporters believe they have to be the first to break the story. After all, isn't that the name of the game?

Many times haste makes for sloppy journalism, and can cause inaccuracies and even loss of purpose. While speaking at Bradford College, Jack Ford, an anchor for ABC television, said, "Competition in the news business is not always good for the consumer. A gravitational pull seems to suck us down to the lowest common denominator."

Ford also criticized cable networks who constantly bring in loud and emotional experts to comment on current events. "Violent talking heads take discussion down a level."

Jeff Wald, News Director of KTLA in Los Angeles reminds us that competition can lead to problems. "There's no journalism in putting a helicopter or press conference on the air just because it's the competitive thing to do."

This is easier said than done. Informed decisions have to be made as to the importance of the event and its significance to the viewer or listener.

When you're live on the air, you're not in control of the pictures and sound. How many times have we seen unruly crowds flashing obscene gestures to a live TV camera, a reporter with a loss for words or a protest at a live press conference? When something is shown on television or heard on the radio that's offensive, the aftermath can be a public relations nightmare. Many times it happened because our competitive natures got the better of us.

In this age of instant, live, breaking news, a broadcast journalist has little time to think before going on the air. It didn't used to be that way. During an interview with the *Columbus Dispatch*, Leslie Stahl remembered:

In the early 1970s, everybody in the country watched network news. There were three options, and we divided up the pie among ourselves.... The U.S. government set their watches to our deadlines—6:30 p.m. at night or, more realistically, 5 p.m., which was our deadline for stories. That was everyone's deadline to finish up their business.

That began to change when CNN came along—ever so slowly. After that, there was this incredible proliferation of broadcast-news sources.

Even as the major networks lost clout, broadcasters in general acquired the ability to go on the air with news in an instant—shrinking "think" time for government officials and reporters alike.

It's that "think time" that's critical to responsible journalism. Hasty writing and decision-making leads to irresponsible actions like releasing names before next of kin are notified, or reporting on serious events based on unverified information heard on the scanner. Think, don't assume or jump to conclusions.

Lily Tomlin may have been more profound than funny when she said, *"The trouble with the rat race is even if you win, you're still a rat."*

Rule Six: Research, Don't Assume

If you don't check your facts, you can't know that they *are* facts. Assumptions can and often do prove to be wrong. After a story is printed or aired, it's too late to verify your information. You end up having to make corrections; you could even find yourself embroiled in a lawsuit. A rule in my newsroom is that a story will not air unless we confirm all information for ourselves or it's attributed to a source that already has.

Misinformation from lack of research or an unreliable source finds its way into newspapers and onto radio and television stations every day. There's no excuse for being sloppy:

- A good newsroom should have a research library with plenty of reference books.
- Reporters should have access to the Internet.
- A manager or producer should double-check the accuracy of a story before it becomes public.

Accuracy is at the very core of sound and responsible journalism, so this is a rule that must *never* be broken.

CHAPTER 2

Responsible Reporting

The reporter is the one who each twenty-four hours dictates the first draft of history.

Douglass Cater

Watch Out for Your Own Mistakes

Every day in every part of the world, reporters make stupid mistakes that inevitably get them into trouble. The overzealous reporter often forgets the rules—and even common sense, for that matter. Here's a story to keep in the back of your mind.

It was just another news day in northern West Virginia when we got a call telling us there was a hostage situation in Preston County. At a drug rehab center, a heavily armed man had taken seven hostages and was holding them at gunpoint. Enter the TV and radio stations. We broke into programming with the details as we became aware of them.

Several hours and a few special reports later, the gunman, still holding the hostages, ordered pizzas to be delivered to the crime scene. The Preston County sheriff decided to dress in street clothes, arm himself and deliver the pizzas. A local radio reporter was doing play-by-play of the entire event for his station from a nearby phone. At this point he proclaimed, live on the air, "The sheriff is getting ready to go in. He's armed with at least three guns and we hope that he will be able to subdue the gunman."

The sheriff entered the building and was greeted by the gunman. Putting a gun to the sheriff's head the gunman said, "Hello, Sheriff. It's nice of you to join us, and thanks for the food." The gunman had been listening to the radio report the entire time. He released the hostages but kept the sheriff at gunpoint. Later that day a television reporter trying to interview to the gunman placed a call to a seldom used phone line in the drug rehab center. The gunman answered the phone and was distracted long enough for the sheriff to apprehend him.

In this case a radio journalist put a person's life in danger through careless reporting. How would you feel if you were the reporter who caused someone great harm?

NEVER report live on behind-the-scenes police activity, or get directly involved in a breaking police investigation.

In this age of live, breaking news, we journalists break this rule every day. How many times have we seen the live pictures of police S.W.A.T. teams moving in on a suspect? What if the person being sought by police is watching television? The suspect will see all the police movements as they are happening. Helicopter journalism is especially disruptive to police activities. Many police departments across the nation have invoked "no-fly policies" when there is a standoff or chase. Other cities, like Los Angeles, are notorious for showing every chase and every standoff.

An incident in Los Angeles further illustrates the danger of reporting on breaking police activity. During the L.A. riots, television stations showed people looting a major discount store. A reporter stated that police were "keeping their distance." This encouraged others to go help loot the store. The reporter made an assumption that the police would not move in and make arrests. The truth was that the police were waiting for reinforcements; when they arrived, the officers moved in and several people were hurt.

Don't Believe the Scanners

Emergency scanner traffic is only an indication of what *may* be going on, and there are as many false alarms as there are actual alerts. Alan Little, a news director in San Antonio, recalled how two of the local stations overreacted to their scanners:

L.A. Riots 1992—Courtesy the Associated Press

We had a situation in November of 1999 when a call came across the scanners about a shooting. The person who reported the incident happened to call from an elementary school. There was an assumption that the shooting had taken place at the school. Two stations (KSAT & KENS) aired that a shooting indeed happened at Coker Elementary. KSAT reported that as many as 16 shoots were fired. In response to that, at least 30 parents rushed to the school to check on their kids. Some even pulled their kids out of school for the day when, in actuality, there had been no shooting at the school. What actually happened was that a custodian on his way to the school got shot at on the freeway—a bullet hit his truck. He called police when he got to Coker Elementary. Wrong information was given out based on the emergency scanner reports.

The lesson: *never report or announce on TV what you hear on emergency scanners unless you confirm it.*

Attribute, Attribute, Attribute

People are convicted by the media every day. Mistakes by reporters, anchors and producers can end up in court, or at least cause a round of nasty phone calls and letters. It can all happen because of one simple word or phrase. But, by attributing the information to an outside source, the reporter can protect the parties involved from liability.

Never be the one to say that someone committed a crime; let someone else say it.

The most responsible way to report a story is to let the witnesses or officials do the talking. Use your sound bites or quotes to tell the story. You become the narrator, so to speak, putting the pieces of the story together in a way that makes sense. The role of a journalist is not to pass judgment, but to report.

When reporting on a person accused of a crime, you must report the outcome of the trial or plea to be fair. Until the matter is resolved legally, always use the term "alleged" to refer to the crimes of which the subject stands accused. While covering a trial, get quotes from each side for every report.

When you use an accusatory sound bite or quote, be sure it's in the proper context.

Many times a person is interviewed about a situation or another person. Be sure that the quote or sound bite you put in your story directly relates to the issue at hand. People are quick to make assumptions and jump to conclusions that may not be correct.

While I was working as a news director in West Virginia, the father of a man who was accused of placing a bomb in a police car sued the TV station for including his name in the report about his son. The father filed the hand-written complaint from his jail cell, as he was already in prison for planting a bomb in a police car a few years before. Nevertheless, the father's and son's cases were indeed separate and the father's complaint had merit.

Be sure the picture or video you use directly corresponds with the story you're telling.

In print, it's the picture above the headline. Make sure the picture is placed carefully, so it's clear with what story it belongs. Ensure, also, that it truly illustrates the subject of your story.

In television, you must never put a person's face on the air if he or she is not directly involved in the story you are telling at that moment. This seems like common sense, but you would be surprised at the number of generic pictures and video clips used every day. If you inadvertently show someone out of context just because you need pictures, you're asking for trouble.

I inherited the following lawsuit when I became news director of a television station that was being sued for misassociation. A family was interviewed for a story about children on the drug Ritalin. Days later, the same reporter was doing an unrelated story about families who have had their children wrongfully diagnosed in order to defraud the federal government. While looking for generic video of children playing, the editor putting together the second story inadvertently used the video of the child from the Ritalin story. The parents from the Ritalin story filed an action, which was later settled after great legal expense.

Remember the rule of attribution.

I like to remember important facts by the use of mnemonic devices. So, here's a way to remember that attribution is the key to staying out of trouble and remaining a responsible journalist. Just like there are two sides to every story, think of the word *PAIRS*:

P   "Police say" ("Officials say," "The District Attorney said," etc.)
A   "Allegedly"
I   "In documents received by this reporter"
R   "Reports by local newspapers indicate" ("Reports by a government agency indicate," etc.)
S   "Suspected of"

It seems elementary, but in haste these words or phases may get left out, causing a reporter to be exposed to legal action. This tends to happen when a producer/writer is in a hurry or is careless. It also happens when reporters and anchors are ad-libbing.

In many of the markets in which I have worked, I have witnessed reporters imply a suspect's guilt by not saying "alleged" or "suspected of." I have also seen defense attorneys ask for a change of venue because a jury may have heard or read the report. There have even been cases in which a newspaper, radio or television station was successfully sued over this, and a suspect who might otherwise have been convicted was found not guilty.

Keep Your Notes

In one case in which I was involved, one of my reporters indicated that a judge had ordered a psychiatric examination for a police officer who was accused of investigating his ex-wife using police computers. The reporter received this information from the ex-wife, confirmed it (off the record) with the judge and never attributed the information. The story was a 20-second voiceover that aired only once.

The officer sued the television station and our reporter for saying on the air that he had had to undergo a mental exam. My general manager and I called the judge and he confirmed that he indeed ordered the exam. Several months went by. The original case against the officer was settled. As part of the settlement, the officer's court records were expunged (destroyed). As the suit against the station progressed, the judge was deposed. He had suffered a stroke since our conversation, and could not remember ordering the exam or talking with my general manager and me. We had no evidence of the truthfulness of our story, so the station's insurance company settled the case.

Even without the court records or the judge's testimony, the station could have beaten the lawsuit if the reporter who filed the story had kept notes demonstrating when and from whom he had received his information. A good rule of thumb is to keep notes and tapes (audio or video) when non-attributed sources have been used. Usually it will become apparent within a few days if an item that has been printed or broadcast will be the subject of a legal protest or become part of an ongoing investigation. If a problem is suspected, *immediately* contact a manager. There are many preventive measures that a news manager, a station manager or a media outlet's legal counsel can take to keep the journalist out of trouble.

Another lesson to be learned from this story: many times it's the simple 20-second story and not the investigative series that will get you into trouble or cause problems. Short stories should be handled with as much care as packages or series pieces.

Subjectivity versus Objectivity

The role of the responsible journalist is to give the facts and let the reader, listener or viewer make the final decision. Fair, objective news coverage is what is preached by news managers across the nation. I always tell my reporters they must get both sides of the story and keep their opinion out of it. The days of Edward R. Murrow are gone (see Chapter 11). Tabloid television shows and newspapers like the *National Enquirer* are where you will find today's subjective writing. The daily newspaper confines subjectivity to the editorial pages, and we rarely see television editorials anymore. Opinionated talk radio is another area of broadcast subjectivity today—ask Rush Limbaugh. Subjective reporting is an oxymoron.

In an interview with Kira Albin of *Grand Times*, Walter Cronkite was asked if he thought people were better off receiving news that's openly subjective so its credibility could be evaluated:

> No, I don't believe that at all. We certainly have subjective columns and editorials. And what we have lost in most newspapers today, and in broadcasting and television, is the editor's column. The editor and publisher, in the old days, had a column, which expressed his or her opinion of affairs. But now we've got the OpEd pages, which are serving the same function and in many ways better, because they express a variety of opinions. That's all for the good.

For the news columns themselves, they certainly should be objective and not subjective. Ten or 15 years ago there was much talk of the new journalism. The philosophy was that since nobody could be 100 percent objective, no one should even try to be objective. And we should all be subjective and tell how stories appear to us, how they affect us personally. That's a bunch of balderdash, and it faded out pretty quickly because it was obviously ridiculous. We must be given the facts so we can make our own judgments, and these facts should not be colored by people's personal opinions....

The mark of a professional journalist is that we do adhere to an ethic. A professional journalist recognizes his or her prejudices and biases and avoids them in writing and reporting. There's no place in journalism for biased reporting on the front page. There is no place for subjective, personal opinions to creep in.

Drawing the Line

Certain stories or aspects of stories should *not* be reported on, either because they could inspire others to take injurious action, or because they expose the innocent or the vulnerable to hurtful public attention.

Suicides

The general rule is, never report a suicide.

As a result of reporting a suicide, vulnerable persons could get the idea that if they commit suicide, their stories would also get on the air or printed in the paper.

The exceptions are:

- **When a public figure takes his or her life.** This includes politicians, celebrities, and anyone else who has been in the public eye. When Marilyn Monroe's body was discovered, it was news. The principle here is that public figures make news by their very actions, no matter how grave.
- **A murder-suicide.** A man in a suburb of Memphis killed his two young sons, laid their bodies in the driveway and then

killed himself next to his sons so his wife would find them when she arrived home. A tragic and true story. When a person is murdered it's obviously news. The fact that the murder happened at the hands of someone who then committed suicide doesn't make it any less newsworthy.

- **A mass suicide.** One day in 1997 the Associated Press flashed this urgent:

> 39 bodies—all white men ages 18 to 24—have been found inside a luxury home in Rancho Santa Fe outside of San Diego, the victims of an apparent mass suicide.
>
> The men, all dressed alike in dark pants and tennis shoes, were found lying prone with their hands at their sides. "There were no signs of trauma," San Diego County Sheriff's Comdr., Alan Fulmer, "The cause of death has not been determined."

A story like this one transcends the suicide rule because of the complex issues that the story itself raises.

Bomb Threats

As a general rule, never report bomb threats.

By reporting a bomb threat, you may be encouraging others to conduct such activities. Police will tell you that in most cases the bomb doesn't exist and a person reported the threat in order to play a prank or get even with someone else.

After the Columbine shootings, a rash of bomb threats were called in to schools throughout the country. In Saint Louis alone there were dozens, and two television stations and one newspaper kept reporting on these threats. It seemed as if the more they reported on threats, the more there were. This prompted me to issue the following statement:

> With the rash of bomb threats at area schools, KDNL-TV (ABC-30) wishes to inform our viewers of our policy regarding the coverage of these type of events.
>
> In a statement issued by ABC-30 News Director Jeff Alan, effective today KDNL-TV WILL NOT report on any bomb threat or threats of violence at any area school. ABC-

30 WILL report any expulsion or arrest resulting from a bomb threat or threat of violence at a school.

"We believe in responsible journalism. Reporting on these types of disruptive actions only encourages this type of behavior," said Alan.

KDNL-TV challenges other broadcasters to take the high road and enact this policy at their stations.

This statement received national attention and was written about in the *New York Times*, the *Christian Science Monitor* and other publications. It seemed elementary!

However, it's easy to lose sight of a policy like this one. Here's how the Associated Press reported on bomb threats that were covered extensively by a Philadelphia television station:

WCAU said Wednesday said it had strayed from its policy on bomb threats while covering the "suburban bomber," a man blamed for more than a dozen real and fake bombs in the area. At least 12 bombs, two of them found last weekend, and four hoaxes have been placed over the last 11 months in shopping center parking lots. Coverage intensified last week as authorities released a composite sketch of the suspect. Stations began breaking into regular programming with news of the latest bomb or suspicious device. WCAU-TV pledged to tone down its coverage of the story. "We felt we had a responsibility to look at how we were covering this story and act in a responsible, mature manner," said Steve Schwaid, vice president of news at the NBC affiliate. "We had our policy in place, and we strayed."

As with suicides, there are exceptions to this rule:

- **When a bomb is actually found.** When a bomb threat leads to the discovery of a suspicious device, that discovery is a legitimate news story.
- **When a bomb threat causes a major evacuation or major public inconvenience.** A shopping mall is evacuated, hundreds of employees are taken from a factory or school children are suddenly sent home without notice. These are examples of when a news organization may consider doing a bomb-threat story. These types of stories should be evaluated

carefully and coverage must be initiated on a case-by-case basis.

Naming Names

Exposing crime victims, innocent bystanders or juveniles has been a problem in our industry for years.

- **Juveniles accused of crimes.** When a nine-year-old gang member was accused of murdering a family, was it right for the media to reveal his name? Some journalists believe that when a juvenile commits a major crime, it's acceptable to reveal the name of the accused to the public. The general rule is to *only reveal the name of a juvenile if he or she is being charged as an adult.*
- **Crime and rape victims.** The rule is, *never expose the identity of a rape victim.* Victims of sexual or violent crimes can be further traumatized by their name or image being shown in a newspaper or on television or mentioned on the radio. Absolutely no purpose is served by exposing the identity of a victim. Rarely, there are occasions when victims come forward and want their story to be told in order for the public to understand what they have been through.

Various states have different laws to protect victims from being exposed to the public. In several states the media is specifically mentioned in these laws, and an example of this is the state of Wyoming. In 2000, A Wyoming judge found KTVQ-TV of Billings, Montana, guilty of contempt for identifying a juvenile victim of sexual assault. The judge imposed a $750 fine, the maximum allowed by law.

One big mistake journalists make without thinking is to expose a juvenile or crime victim by referring to another person involved in the story. "John Doe was outraged that the prosecutor dropped the rape charges involving the alleged crime against his daughter." Statements like this slip into newspaper articles and broadcasts all the time. This is sloppy, irresponsible journalism, plain and simple.

As a responsible journalist, be aware of any potential harm that may be inflicted upon others by your story. There can be exceptions to rules, but in general:

- When using a victim's name in a story, ask a news manager or producer for advice.

- Never use a victim's name without the victim's approval.
- Never accidentally identify a victim through association.
- Treat rape and other sexual crimes with extra sensitivity.
- Never identify murder victims unless officials have released the names to the media.
- Before using a name, consider the potential for harm to a person's reputation.

Crossing the Line

It's natural for journalists to want to become involved in their story, but they can't, and this is a temptation that's very hard to resist. Many of the stories we tell as journalists would make good fiction—the only problem is, they're true. The following is an extraordinary example, the account of a reporter in Tampa who broke the story of a state attorney accused of using other people's money to gamble. How the story unfolded and how the reporter became personally involved is reminiscent of a TV movie.

In order to show the contrast between how this story was reported to the public by the local newspaper and what actually happened at WFLS-TV, here's the newspaper article in its entirely, followed by the candid commentary of WFLS-TV news director Dan Bradley.

We begin with the newspaper story by Eric Deggans of the *Saint Petersburg Times:*

Steve Andrews wants people to know one thing: He's not emotionally distraught.

He has had good reason. Andrews, the lead reporter in WFLA-Ch. 8's Target 8 investigative unit, broke the story of Hillsborough State Attorney Harry Lee Coe. Coe had borrowed thousands of dollars from employees in his office and then attempted to cover up visits to hundreds of gambling sites over the Internet via an office computer.

In April, Andrews notified the Florida Department of Law Enforcement when he suspected the state attorney altered a document showing which Web sites he had visited. In July, when Gov. Jeb Bush ordered a full investigation and Coe killed himself, it was Andrews who found the body.

Steve Andrews (right), with producer/photographer Gordon Dempsey—
Courtesy WFLA-TV

But as he sat in a comfortable office at WFLA's new headquarters last week, the veteran reporter seemed the picture of composure.

"While it was a sad turn of events, I wasn't devastated," he says of finding Coe's body slumped beneath an overpass of the Lee Roy Selmon Expressway, while trying to track down the state attorney for a response to Bush's decision. "I don't mean to sound cold, but the first (dead) body I ever saw left more of an impression."

Andrews' call to the FDLE had prompted the agency to investigate Coe's gambling activities and debts. So, he said, "I knew there was a portion of the (TV) audience that would blame me."

But there is another concern: that Andrews' call to the FDLE crossed a thin line between reporting the news and influencing it.

It's a view shared by some journalism experts, who say such actions turn journalists into agents of the police.

"There's a danger there, and a not inconsequential one, that the public begins to view reporters as an arm of law enforcement," said Carl Gottlieb, deputy director of the Washington D.C.–based Project for Excellence in Journalism.

"In a business where perception is reality, for the public to perceive that a news outlet is either an arm of or works hand-in-hand with the police is a little troubling," said the former TV news executive with 20 years' experience in the business. "It's dangerous for all of us."

For the public, it might seem a simple issue. If a citizen believes a crime has been committed—particularly by the county's most powerful law enforcement officer—isn't it his duty to tell police?

But journalists aren't ordinary citizens. Andrews defends the decision to call the FDLE, pushed by vice president of news Dan Bradley, saying the station had reached an impasse in their reporting and was afraid Coe would destroy evidence of his Internet gambling before WFLA could confirm enough details to air a story.

Armed with Coe's own user name and password for a gambling site he visited, Andrews said he called FDLE officials in April and asked them to investigate whether Coe was gambling over the Internet and borrowing heavily from employees to cover losses.

FDLE officials say they had sporadic contact with Andrews after that first conversation and never promised they would give him advance notice of any findings or official action. (Last week, the agency issued a report confirming Andrews' stories.)

Andrews never revealed his sources, which he said, were "deep inside (Coe's) office."

Charles Guthrie, supervisor of the FDLE's white-collar crimes division, said he can't remember the last time a reporter called specifically to request an investigation.

"(We kept) a very arm's-length relationship... I never even met the guy until (last week)," Guthrie said. "It was a call out of the blue."

It would be weeks later, on July 10, that Andrews would break his first story: that Coe borrowed $12,000 from two employees in his office. On July 12, Andrews reported their contact with the FDLE and Bush's order to begin the investigation, showing footage of Coe denying the allegations about betting via the Internet.

The next day, while waiting in front of Coe's apartment, Andrews and photographer Gordon Dempsey noticed a slumped figure nearby. After seeing blood on the figure's shirt, they looked closer and discovered who it was.

"I thought, 'Why did it have to be me (who found him)?'" Andrews said. He agreed to work off-camera in reporting on Coe's death that week once Bradley and other WFLA executives concluded "we didn't want to be perceived as kicking a dead man."

But negative calls and e-mail poured into the station from viewers who blamed the media in general, and WFLA specifically, for hounding Coe to his death. One person even threatened to show up at Andrews' home.

"Even now, people ask 'How do you feel?'...and I'm tired," said Andrews, 47, an employee at WFLA for 15 years. "I've worked a lot of hours and taken a lot of heat."

This wasn't the first time Andrews had given a heads up to law enforcement while investigating allegations of criminal activity.

"We have every bit as much responsibility to report wrongdoing as the next person," said Bradley, WFLA's vice president of news. "If we have knowledge that a crime is taking place, we should report it. And we can do that several ways...either through our reporting or by calling (law enforcement) directly."

For Gary Hill, head of the investigative team at KSTP-TV in Minneapolis and co-chair of the Society of Professional Journalists' ethics committee, the key is independence. Was WFLA's reporting independent from the law enforcement investigation?

"You don't want to go to a (police) station and say, "Here's our files...let us know when you do a bust,' " Hill said. "(But) it sounds like (WFLA) did a real public service in reporting this."

Gottlieb, at the Project for Excellence in Journalism, disagrees, saying such practices could lead potential sources to conclude, "if what I'm going to tell you will land on the desk of law enforcement, maybe I won't tell you anything."

At least, Andrews and WFLA are up-front about their contacts with law enforcement. But, hard as it is to argue the unmasking of Coe's misdeeds, I can't help thinking that too much cooperation with police leads journalists to become part of the story they're covering.

But I—and others who've criticized WFLA's call to FDLE—believe the station should not be blamed for Coe's suicide.

"We want reporters to be dogged, and sometimes the outcome is going to be unfortunate," Gottlieb said. "There are times the outcome is tough to foresee and even tougher to take. But that's our job."

Although Andrews and Bradley avoid using the word "vindication," they admit it was a high point when the FDLE later confirmed their stories.

"This is why I got into news," Andrews said. "We had information that a public official was breaking the law and we exposed it. That's what journalism is all about."

The *St. Petersburg Times* placed the issue of WFLA-TV's direct involvement in this story before the public. First was the question of whether or not the reporter should have notified law enforcement prior to the airing of this story. News director Dan Bradley explains why, in his mind, there was no other choice:

We were at a point where we had a lot of information but we were not comfortable enough to go on the air and publish it. We knew records existed and they had blocked us from every angle. We knew that there was clear evidence that within the Office of the State Attorney, if not illegal, certainly highly questionable and unethical practices were taking place. What we didn't have was information that there was direct corruption connected to Coe's gambling addiction. We talked about it, we struggled with it, and we decided that we didn't have enough information for a story. We knew a crime may have taken place; so, like any other citizen we felt we had an obligation to share what we knew with a state criminal investigation agency that specializes in government corruption.

The story aired, and it was picked up by both of the local newspapers. The governor called for a special investigation and, on the morning after, every television news outlet and newspaper had reporters and photographers at the courthouse waiting for Coe's arrival. Steve Andrews, the reporter who broke the story, called Dan Bradley and, after waiting well past the time Coe usually arrives at work, was convinced that he most likely wasn't going to show. Andrews let Bradley know that he was going to leave the courthouse and try to locate him.

Bradley describes what happened next:

Andrews knew some of the places Coe frequented. They went to Coe's apartment and saw his car, so they assumed he was there. They waited off property and saw an investigator come by and look in the windows of the apartment. The investigator approached Andrews and asked what he was doing. The reporter said they were looking for Coe; the investigator said, "We are, too." Andrews and his photographer decided to circle the block and then go to another location where Coe might have been. While stopped at a traffic light a block from the apartment, they saw a slumped body under an expressway overpass. They thought it was a homeless person. They got out of the car and when they got within ten feet they immediately knew it was Coe. They saw the blood on his head. The photographer jumped on his cell phone and called 911. Andrews called the assignment desk. They chased me down and, very distraught, told me what Andrews had found. I said, don't touch anything. I asked if he had his camera out, and if he had taken pictures? Andrews said no and I told him *do not* take any pictures; get back in your car and wait for the police.

At this point all I could think of was that we (WFLA-TV) were right in the middle of a story. We were no longer covering the story; we were part of it. I immediately knew that despite what we knew about suicide and why it happens, there was going to be a huge outcry in the community that we had killed Harry Lee Coe. I had two things in mind at that point: I need to slow this news organization down so that it doesn't make any mistakes, and I need to get Steve Andrews out of there because his role has changed from reporter to participant. When it heard the police call on the scanners, the assignment desk dispatched the helicopter, three live trucks and two more reporters. It was classic pandemonium at the assignment desk. I said, okay, everybody stop, slow down. Number one, we're miles ahead of everyone with this story and it's not necessarily a story we need to win as much as it's a story we need to do right. I ordered the helicopter back; the assignment editor questioned why. I asked, when was the last time you dispatched the helicopter to cover a suicide? I made an announcement. Everybody listen, at this moment, until this story shifts again, we are coving a suicide. We have guidelines for how we cover a suicide.

I then went to the scene. I asked the police to release my reporter and photographer from the scene. I agreed to let them both be questioned later and handed the police my card.

When we all arrived back at the station I was concerned about them being emotionally disturbed by what had happened. On the one hand your defense mechanism goes up as a reporter, but on the other hand either one of them could be thinking, oh my God, I killed this guy. We talked and they declined any counseling. I asked Andrews not to report the story on that day. I worried how he would be perceived by the viewers who liked Harry Lee Coe, who couldn't help but to think Andrews had killed him. Those people could see you as being on the air bragging about what you did. I thought we needed to put a layer of separation between Andrews and the story for the next few days. He agreed. I also cut Andrews off from several interview requests from other media. I sat in on the debriefing of my crew by the detectives and kept notes. The newspaper editors demanded to talk with Andrews. The point I made to them was, if this were your reporter who had made this discovery, would you make that reporter available to be interviewed by the other media? I explained that my job as news director is to look out for the journalism of the story, the welfare of my newsroom and the welfare of two reporters who are emotionally distraught.

WFLA-TV was *not* the first station to cut into programming with a special report about Coe's death. WFLA-TV waited for conformation that next of kin had been notified before they put the story on the air.

Following are some key elements to this incredible story that no journalist should ever forget:

- When you get personally involved in a story, always seek the help of others to keep the story in perspective.
- If you come upon a crime scene or a suicide, don't touch anything, and call the police.
- Don't rush to report a death of any kind. You do not want next of kin finding out about the tragedy from you.
- Seek counseling if you feel the story has had a major emotional impact on you.
- Do not talk to other media without consulting your editor or news director.
- When in a situation like this one, don't make competitive decisions—make journalistic decisions.

This story was not the first in which the subject of an investigation took his own life. People can reach a personal breaking point, sometimes spurred on by media in a feeding frenzy. A state official shot himself on live television during a hearing into his alleged wrongdoing. A jeweler accused of filling in flawed diamonds with glue and selling them as flawless killed himself when a local television station became relentless with the story.

So, how much is enough? Whenever possible, a reporter should make an assessment of a story's potential impact. If there are indicators that the subject of the story is unstable, extra care should be taken. In reality, a reporter may have no way of knowing, but it's always a good idea to keep the potential for tragedy in mind.

Sometimes the line between responsible and irresponsible journalism is blurry. Patrick Emory reported television news at the local and national level for more than three decades. He knows how fine this line can be.

By definition, a journalist takes it upon him or herself to inform the public of events and machinations in society.

The journalist must apply some kind of yardstick of responsibility. Examples: 1: "Mother Nature was kind to us this year, and we have a bumper corn crop in our county." 2: "Farmer Jones was caught adding weight to his bushels and was fined." 3: "County agriculture commissioner Smith was seen taking an envelope from Farmer Jones. Smith made a personal bank deposit of five thousand dollars. He hadn't won anything and no relatives had died. Farmer Jones' earlier fine was reduced by Commissioner Smith." All three lines contain truths and fact. But is number three responsible reporting?

We all know the stories of journalists and presidents. Lincoln, Roosevelt, Kennedy and even George Bush were reportedly less than faithful to their wives. But did anyone actually witness the potential infidelities?

Clinton was forced to admit it. But, more importantly, were the journalists of years ago more responsible for not reporting the rumors? Did those stories have any bearing on the job the president was doing?

I was directly involved in a situation in which I was accused of being irresponsible and it was used against me. I placed a phone call into a hostage situation in Florida and aired an interview with the hostage taker, contrary to instructions from the news director. A radio reporter had done the same thing. My motives were to advance the story and beat the competition. The hostage was never harmed. True, this guy had killed three cops, but he swore he had no intention of hurting the woman hostage. He eventually let her go and put a bullet through his head. I hung up very quickly after getting the guy on the phone. But, years in the journalism business had driven me to keep going for more "news." I later felt my efforts were used against me by the management. Was what I did irresponsible? I maintain it was not, especially after the radio reporter had aired his interview over the phone. But, I can see and understand legitimate criticism of what I did and what the radio reporter did. The radio reporter's actions became a point of much debate in the journalism community. My connection with the hostage taker never became public. Did the radio reporter's interview endanger the hostage? Debatable.

Another criticism was that police trying to contact the hostage taker ran into trouble on the phone line because of calls placed by reporters to the store. I disagree because the police would have had no trouble getting the phone company to clear the line of any conversation so they could make contact. I will admit to some uneasiness over what I did but I would not concede that what I did was "irresponsible."

What I do find to be less than responsible has nothing to do with the life and death part of this story. It is the scramble for ratings that causes some so-called journalists to produce vacuous pieces and tie them in pretty ribboned packages for the sole purpose of attracting viewers during ratings periods. I'm not suggesting all ratings efforts are vacuous, but we all know that a good portion of them are, in fact, of no particular value. Much more effort is put into the packaging and promoting of some of these efforts than into the substance of the reporting. That is irresponsible.

The demonstrations of "story propriety" outlined here go to the core of responsible decision making. WFLA-TV made responsible decisions while covering a story in which it *unintentionally* became directly involved when its reporter discovered the suicide of one of his story subjects. Yet, the public reaction that followed was less than flattering. A reporter calling into a hostage situation cannot be condoned because in this case, he or she would *intentionally* become part of the story.

There is a pronounced difference between reporting on and becoming part of any story—especially when it deals with matter of life and death.

> *A man who is good for anything ought not to calculate the chance of living or dying; he ought only to consider whether in doing anything he is right or wrong—acting the part of a good man or of a bad.*
>
> Socrates

CHAPTER 3

The Hidden Truth

Truth is stranger than fiction.

Mark Twain

What Lies Beneath...

There are always stories behind the stories. There are also stories that aren't apparent on the surface.... Literally!

Look at the picture of this church. It looks like any other church, but there is one important difference. Reporter Jean Jackson of KDNL-TV filed the following report:

THIS MAY LOOK LIKE A NORMAL CHURCH, BUT THERE'S SOMETHING HIDDEN INSIDE THE STEEPLE.

[BRYCE MOSHER/CIS COMMUNICATIONS]
"THEY STILL WANT TO USE THEIR PHONES, THEY JUST DON'T WANT TO SEE THE ANTENNAS."

AND NOWADAYS, YOU CAN'T. SEE THE TOP OF THAT OFFICE BUILDING BEHIND HIM?

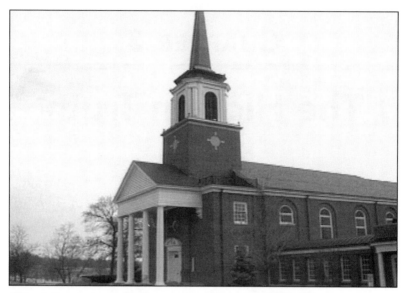

Church Steeple is a cell phone tower—Courtesy KDNL-TV

INSIDE, IT HOLDS NINE CELLULAR TELEPHONE ANTEN-
NAS ON PANELS THAT REACH CELLULAR CUSTOMERS IN
A TWO-MILE RADIUS.

IT'S CALLED A STEALTH TOWER, AND THEY'RE POPPING
UP ALL OVER THE ST. LOUIS AREA.

[STANDUP]
"COMMUNICATIONS COMPANIES HAVE HAD TO GET
PRETTY CRAFTY TO HIDE TRANSMISSION TOWERS.
THEY'VE USED FLAG POLES, LIGHTPOLES, EVEN
STEEPLES. TRY TO FIND THE CELLULAR TRANSMISSION
TOWER IN THE STEEPLE BEHIND ME."

[TRACK]
THE TRANSMISSION LINES ARE HIDDEN IN THE RECTAN-
GULAR COLUMNS, ADDED TO THE EXISTING STEEPLE
STRUCTURE.

[BRYCE MOSHER]
"THE STEALTH TECHNOLOGY HAS BEEN ADVANCING
OVER THE YEARS; WE'VE BEEN COMING OUT WITH MORE

Cross is a cell phone antenna—Courtesy KDNL-TV

AND MORE WAYS TO HIDE ANTENNAS. THE MOST RE-
CENT ONE I FOUND WAS OFF OF ST. CHARLES ROCK
ROAD AND OFF MCKELVEY. IT IS A CROSS THAT IS BASI-
CALLY AN ANTENNA STRUCTURE."

"IT JUST LOOKS LIKE A GIANT WHITE CROSS."

[TRACK]
AND THE POWER OF THE CROSS BENEFITS BOTH THE
CELLULAR CUSTOMERS, AND THE CHURCH WHICH RE-
CEIVES MONTHLY PAYMENTS FOR THE USE OF THE
STRUCTURE.

THERE'S A CELLULAR TRANSMITTER ATOP THE ST. LOUIS
SCIENCE CENTER, AND ANOTHER NEXT DOOR AT ST.
LOUIS UNIVERSITY HIGH SCHOOL.

THIS STEALTH TECHNOLOGY ISN'T CHEAP...OFTEN FIVE TO
TEN TIMES THE COST OF A TRADITIONAL TRANSMITTER.

BUT IT'S WORTH IT TO CELLULAR COMPANIES TRYING TO
MEET THE GROWING NEEDS OF CELLULAR USERS.

This story came to the attention of one of my reporters who had learned that cell phone companies were using churches and schools to hide cell phone antennas. When the idea was pitched in our morning meeting, everyone in the room was amazed. The reaction immediately told me this was a good story.

The cell phone company was more than happy to take us around town and show us their handiwork.

Following Through

We then asked the question, "Is there any danger?" After all, these transmitters were in churches and schools—a good investigative report for another day. Whenever you report story number one, look for story number two or three. A good practice is to keep a notebook that's both a reminder and a story log. You can refer to it on slow news days and often become a hero in your editorial meeting.

Look carefully at the picture below, which I took during a visit to Key West.

You see a dog with a cat on its back and two white mice on the cat.

Here's what you don't see.

Photo by Jeff Alan

The truth here lies beneath the cat. There's a harness around the dog holding the cat in place. The mice are tied to the top of the cat. These animals' owner used human curiosity to solicit money. He had a sign that read, take as many pictures as you like for one dollar.

If I had been a reporter doing a story, I would have put together a great little feature story on this and probably never followed through. But if I had gone back to check on these animals the next day, they would not have been there. Instead I would have found that the man was showing a picture of the cat around town in an effort to find it. I would have learned that the cat had had enough, eaten the mice and run away. I could also have explored the question of animal abuse. There's always more to a story.

Human curiosity can always be promoted and reported on. The tunnels under your city, the secret recipe of a local restaurant or the origins of a statue in a town square. It's what you can't see and the curiosity of what's not readily apparent that makes for solid and interesting responsible journalism.

> *Set your sights beyond what you can see. There is true majesty in the concept of an unseen power which can neither be measured nor weighed.*
>
> Ted Koppel

Finding Out the Truth

One of the best ways of getting at the truth on governmental matters is the *Freedom of Information Act* (FOIA). This act makes information from federal agencies available to the public. The American Civil Liberties Union (*www.ACLU.org*) provides a primer on how to use it. Here is an excerpt:

Any Person Can Make A FOIA Request

The FOIA permits "any person" to request access to agency records. "Any person" includes—

- U.S. citizens
- Permanent resident aliens
- Foreign nationals

- Corporations and unincorporated associations
- Universities
- State and local governments and members of Congress

A Quick Response Required

The FOIA requires an agency to decide within ten working days whether to comply with a FOIA request and to inform the person making the request of the decision and of the person's right to appeal a refusal to provide information to the head of the agency. An agency has 20 days to respond to an administrative appeal. If it upholds the decision to refuse to provide the information, it must inform the person requesting it of the right to appeal to a federal court.

An agency may take an additional ten days to respond to the initial request or the appeal under "unusual circumstances." This usually means the agency has to get the records from its field offices, or has to process a large volume of separate records, or it has to consult with another agency, or two or more of its components in order to satisfy your request.

Planning Your Strategy

Here are some tips for planning your FOIA request—

- Try to limit your request to what you really want. If you simply ask for "all files relating to" a particular subject (including yourself), you may give the agency an excuse to delay its response, and you risk needlessly running up search and copying costs.
- If you know that your request involves a great volume of records, try to state both what your request includes and what it does not include.
- Be as specific as possible. Cite relevant newspaper clips, articles, congressional reports, etc. If the records have already been released, let the agency know the date, release number, and name of the original requester.

- Let the agency know if you'd like to receive information in a particular order. Materials could be reviewed and released to you in chronological or geographical order—or you may simply not want to wait for all the records to be reviewed before any are released.

The U.S. government has put this tool at the reporter's disposal and it's a good one. Remember that the production of documents can come with a hefty price tag for research and copying. Always ask what the FOIA request will cost you.

FOIA requests are limited to certain types of documents. If a document contains personal information like medical history, or its release could damage national security, it is exempt from the FOIA.

A local news director recalls how one of his reporters took the Freedom of Information Act too far:

An anchor/reporter I hired was great on-air but a little light in common sense and knowledge of reporting and journalism. She was doing a story on city government and how business was frequently conducted at private lunches with multiple city employees, board members and elected officials...to get around open meeting laws.

But the community's movers and shakers influenced decisions by having lunches at one of two private clubs in town. She wanted the invoices and billing records...and made quite a scene when she was asked to leave. The phone call from the GM hit my office before she got back to the newsroom.

I had to explain in some detail to her about FOIA and open records and how they just didn't apply in most cases to private citizens. You just can't walk up to somebody and say, "Show me your club bills because I'm a reporter."

Investigate and Make an Impression

Journalists can and often do make a difference. After all, finding the truth is our job. Good journalism can be a product of enterprise, or it can spring from our own experiences. A great example of an impressive piece of reporting comes from Laurie Stein, an anchor-reporter for WPLG-TV in Miami:

Courtesy WPLG-TV

A few years ago, my sister was at a hotel with my nephew. When she requested a crib for her room, she was shocked to see what shape it was in—rickety, old, unstable. She mentioned this to me, and I sort of filed it away in my "things wrong with the world that should someday be looked into" part of my brain.

About a year later I became the "consumer investigator" for WPLG-TV in Miami, Florida. I was constantly under pressure to come up with great ideas for investigations, and I pitched this idea to my news director: let's go into several hotels, request cribs, and see what we get.

I did some research and found that 50 children die in unsafe cribs each year; I also found a child who was brain-damaged after a worn-out hotel crib collapsed on him. We found a safety expert and brought him from hotel to hotel as we quickly checked in, inspected the cribs, and moved to the next hotel. Almost all the cribs were in terrible shape according to the expert, potential death traps with worn-out and bent hardware, huge gaps that could suffocate a child, broken parts, large pieces of wood splintering apart, etc. These were mostly obvious problems that should have been noticed by the hotel.

The tricky part was finding someone from each hotel who could immediately respond to our allegations. (I stress "immediately," because I wanted to see what they would say to a customer, on the spot, not in an official corporate response days later.) At each hotel, I phoned the front desk, said I was a reporter for Channel 10 and asked for "a manager, or anyone who represents the hotel" to come to our room because "there was a problem with the crib." Then it was all about ambushing. As soon as they came to the room, the camera was on and I fired out the questions: "Did you know this crib was defective?"; "Do you inspect your cribs before giving them to customers?"

The reactions made for great television, very spontaneous. We were putting these people on camera, without much warning. Most hemmed and hawed and stumbled out a response about how they had no idea the cribs were in such bad shape, and they didn't know they were dangerous. One night manager had a very bizarre reaction to the questions and the camera—he looked into the camera and said, "Hey, I'm gonna give a shout-out to my boys in Miami—what's up... Hey, I'm gonna dance for the camera..." etc. Obviously, thinking if he acted crazy then we'd air none of his strange responses to our very serious questions. However, we aired all of it. In fact, I ended the story with him making a sarcastic comment about customer service at his hotel.

Many people asked me why I included that response, especially in such a serious story. The news director looked at my script and said, "What is this?" Our attorney, who must approve all investigative scripts, could not understand it at all—and I had to really fight to include it. I felt that his behavior explained exactly the point I was making: many of these hotels did not take the issue seriously. Also, I had asked the hotel for a representative who speaks for the hotel...just because the response doesn't come from corporate honcho with an official-sounding explanation doesn't mean it's not valid for our story. His response was his response, and I didn't want to cover that up. I just wouldn't give up; I kept stressing my feelings to the news director and the attorney. Finally they relented.

Years later, everyone remembers the obnoxious guy in the hotel cribs story. And the story prompted the consumer products safety commission to devise new guidelines for hotels; it also convinced the Florida hotel and motel association to alert all lodging establishments to check their cribs. I also showed the story to a Florida senator, who sponsored a bill on hotel crib safety that just passed its first committee in the house.

The aftermath of good investigative stories can help people and communities, reverse injustices, and create new hopes and dreams. From the simplest story to a five part investigative series, newspapers and radio and television stations throughout the world strive to uncover the truth, and sometimes actually help to correct problems.

A simple "good story test" is to ask these questions before you proceed:

- How would I react to this story as a reader, listener or viewer?
- What is the potential positive outcome if I do this story responsibly?
- Is there a potential downside to doing this story?
- Will this story hurt anyone?

An example of a story that easily passes this test comes from Mindy Basara, an anchor and reporter for WBAL-TV in Baltimore:

I recently did an investigation into the conditions of city playgrounds. We found dangerous levels of lead-based paint that was chipping off. This exposed children to a health hazard. After the story ran, the city spent one million dollars replacing playground equipment.

There may be a playground like this one in your city. Hundreds of positive changes to our communities happen every year as a direct result of responsible journalism. In the Saint Louis City Schools, a report on the hazards of asbestos caused a school to be closed and thousands of students to be tested. Speeding laws were enforced following a report on speeders near schools, and highways were rebuilt after a report on numerous fatal accidents.

Tell the Truth

A reporter's duty is to be careful that the truth is actually the truth. Just because someone says something happened doesn't make it so. Careless journalists give us all a bad name.

In a speech, Cokie Roberts, co-anchor of the ABC news program *This Week* and an analyst with National Public Radio, said she has concluded that much of the criticism of the media is "that people think we don't care." And when reporters are not careful with small facts, she said, readers and viewers come to question the accuracy of the entire news report.

"We're not careful," said Roberts. "There's a carelessness about facts; there's a carelessness about fairness; there's a carelessness about writing."

Always check your work. Don't rush to judgment. In a business in which deadlines loom like a black cloud over your head all the time, don't make a stupid mistake for the sake of time.

Use caution when a deadline is approaching and make sure that what is about to be printed or aired is the truth. If you're not sure, don't let a co-worker talk you into running something that will come back to haunt you later. Always look ahead and be your own worst critic!

Let's face it: we all make mistakes. If you make an error in judgement, analyze the extent of your mistake and learn how to prevent a similar mistake in the future. We are often judged as "the media" with little regard to the individual who made the mistake. Sam Donaldson wishes the general public could read this book:

The general public doesn't have any interest or time to do that I suppose. If they did they would know more about what we try to do.

It's always been interesting to me that when we make mistakes, which we do, there's a segment of the public that immediately jumps to the conclusion that we've done that on purpose. Usually because we have some evil agenda of our own.

I say to people if you go to a dentist and you say, I've got a toothache, and the guy starts drilling in the wrong tooth, you don't jump out of the chair and say it's a conspiracy of dentists. You say, you idiot, you drilled the wrong tooth.

If the general public would read a book like this, I think it would help them understand that we care about the business and we work very hard to do it right. And sometimes we don't do it right, for which we should hang our heads. If you deal with professional people who know the rules and know why they're important you're going to get a better shot at getting information that is accurate and responsible.

In general, if you tell the truth without embellishment in the course of reporting a story, there can be no intent to commit harm. That's what attorneys look for when they advise clients on whether or not to sue.

As long as you truly believe your story is accurate and relevant, your journalistic integrity will remain intact.

CHAPTER 4

Responsible Broadcasting

The Medium Is the Message.

Marshall McLuhan

Good Journalism = Good Ratings

Broadcast journalists have always heard the phase, "Never bury the lead." What about, "Never bury the lead story"? Producers tend to lead with the big story of the day, but consider the alternative. Generally, if four television stations' late newscasts all lead with the exact same story, same press conference and same interviews, the audience will either gravitate to the number one station, or stay with the station with the best lead-in. A station can break out of this pattern and attract more viewers by leading with a story that sets it apart from its competitors. In an unscientific study based on the Nielsen overnights in Saint Louis, the station with the compelling alternative lead has a higher-than-normal rating.

On an average news day, as a producer or news manager looks for a story that's exclusive or qualifies to be the lead, he or she should consider not leading with the obvious story. If you have local breaking news or a major national story, of course it's your lead, but for every "breaking news day" there are two other days when you could dare to be different.

Case in point: It was a night in early 2000. The lead story on all the other stations was a police chase. We made the decision to lead with an investigative story. Nurses and doctors stood by and watched a man die because he signed a "do not resuscitate" order—or did he?

Here's the script from reporter Paul Brown:

"WE WERE MARRIED IN 1951"

JAMES MARKHAM WAS A 74-YEAR-OLD HUSBAND, FATHER AND A WORLD WAR TWO VETERAN. ON JANUARY 16TH HE LAY DYING AT A V.A. NURSING HOME BUT THE DOC-TORS AND NURSES DIDN'T DO ANYTHING TO SAVE HIM.

[SOUNDBITE SUSAN MARKHAM]
SUSAN MARKHAM/VICTIM'S DAUGHTER

"THE DOCTOR CAME IN AND SAID I DIDN'T DO ANY-THING BECAUSE YOU KNOW YOUR DAD WAS DNR. AND I WENT NUTS."

[SOUNDBITE MARY MARKHAM]
MARY MARKHAM/WIFE

Courtesy KDNL-TV

"I DIDN'T EVEN KNOW WHAT DNR MEANT."

[GRAPHIC]
DNR. DO NOT RESCUSITATE. A DNR ORDER WAS PUT
INTO MARKHAM'S FILE WITHOUT THE FAMILY'S KNOWL-
EDGE OR CONSENT.

[SOUNDBITE SUSAN]
"ALTHOUGH HE HAD PARKINSON'S AND MULTIPLE MED-
ICAL PROBLEMS HE HAD A QUALITY OF LIFE THAT WAS
ACCEPTABLE TO HIM. HE WAS NOT IN PAIN, HE WAS NOT
UNHAPPY AND HE SMILED."

[STAND UP]
JAMES MARKHAM'S FAMILY WANTED HIM TO LIVE AND
THEY THINK THAT'S WHAT HE WANTED TOO. THAT'S WHY
THEY'RE OUTRAGED THAT A SOCIAL WORKER AND A
DOCTOR HERE AT THE V.A. HOSPITAL CHANGED HIS MED-
ICAL STATUS FROM A PATIENT WHO WOULD GET LIFE
SAVING TREATMENT, TO DO NOT RECUSITATE. THEY SAY
HE WASN'T COMPETENT TO MAKE THAT LIFE OR DEATH
DECISION HIMSELF.

[GRAPHIC MEDICAL RECORDS—VIDEO]
ONE DOCTOR'S NOTES FROM THE DAY THE DNR ORDER
WAS ISSUED SHOW MARKHAM WAS "DEMENTED,"
"UNRESPONSIVE" TO QUESTIONS AND "UNABLE TO
COMMUNICATE."

[GRAPHIC MED RECORDS]
BUT LATER THE SAME DAY A SOCIAL WORKER WROTE
SHE "DISCUSSED THE ISSUE AT LENGTH" WITH MARKHAM
AND HE "WANTED TO BE DNR."

[SOUNDBITE SUSAN]
"HE HAD PARKINSONS DISEASE. SHE SAID HE NODDED
HIS HEAD. HE NODDED HIS HEAD ALL THE TIME."

BUT WHAT REALLY GETS THE FAMILY IS THAT THEY WERE
NEVER CONSULTED.

[SOUNDBITE JIM MARKHAM]
JIM MARKHAM/SON

"IF THEY HAD COME TO US AND SAID THERE IS JUST NO HOPE, WE MAY HAVE ALL MADE THE DECISION, BUT WE DIDN'T GET THAT CHANCE. EVIDENTLY SOMEONE ELSE MADE IT FOR US."

[SOUNDBITE DR. GRIFFIN TROTTER]
DR. GRIFFIN TROTTER/ETHICS PROFESSOR

"DO THEY HAVE REASON TO BE UPSET? DO THEY NOT HAVE A REASON TO BE UPSET? IT'S HARD TO SAY."

DR. GRIFFIN TROTTER IS A MEDICAL ETHICS PROFESSOR. HE DOESNT THINK THERE IS ALWAYS A CLEAR-CUT ANSWER WHEN IT COMES TO DETERMINING WHEN A PATIENT SHOULD BE A DNR.

[SOUNDBITE DR TROTTER]
"I BELIEVE THERE WILL ALWAYS BE CONTROVERSIAL CASES THAT THERE IS NO PROCEDURE OR PROCEDURAL ETHIC OR WAY OF DOING THINGS THAT IS GOING TO GUARANTEE THAT THE DECISION MAKING WILL ALWAYS HAVE THE INTEGRITY THAT WE ALL WANT."

THE FAMILY PLANS TO FIND OUT IN A WRONGFUL DEATH LAWSUIT EXACTLY WHAT THE CORRECT PROCEDURE IS. THE V.A. DEFENDS ITS TREATMENT OF MARKHAM WITH THIS STATEMENT RELEASED TO ABC 30 NEWS.

[GRAPHIC]
"V.A. OFFERS THE FAMILY ITS SINCERE SYMPATHY ON THE LOSS OF THEIR LOVED ONE."

"THE HEALTHCARE PROFESSIONALS RESPONSIBLE FOR MR. MARKHAM'S CARE FOLLOWED ALL ACCREDITATION REQUIREMENTS AND V.A. REGULATIONS."

[SOUNDBITE SUSAN]
"I THINK IT'S A COVER UP. I THINK THEY KNOW THEY SCREWED UP ROYALLY..."

JAMES MARKHAM WAS BURIED AT JEFFERSON BARRACKS. HIS FAMILY KNEW THIS IS WHERE HE WOULD EVENTUALLY END UP. THEY JUST WISH THEY WOULD HAVE HAD THE CHANCE TO TELL HIM

When the ratings came in the next day, our station delivered a rating 40 percent higher than the average for that night of the week.

The Responsible Newscast

Don't just look at the lead story; look at the broadcast as a whole. It's the neatly wrapped package that makes or breaks a radio or television station. Every element counts, including your treatment of national news, your local weather, sports, and even the kicker. Lynn Heider, news director of WEWS-TV in Cleveland, shares her thoughts on the "great, responsible" newscast:

A "great newscast" is compelling, responsible, informative, thought-provoking, empowering, disconcerting and comfortable all at once. It *compels* people to watch, because the content is consistently good. Viewers are taken on a roller coaster ride of emotions, given front row seats at history-making events, introduced to the world's most interesting people—both ordinary and extraordinary—treated to exciting pictures, allowed to hear incredible voices, and given time to laugh and cry.

It is *responsible* in that it takes ownership of the communities it serves. It rights wrongs, exposes problems, explores solutions and crusades for people who do not have a voice elsewhere. The responsibility taken by a great news team fits the Poynter model for excellence; it minimizes harm and weighs carefully the purpose of sensitive material.

It is *informative* because, ideally, it is a true reflection of what life was like in that particular market. The stories are not overblown examples of the atypical but rather mirrors of events in the communities the television station is serving. That informative newscast helps people spend their money wisely, decide how to vote, raise their children and choose what to do for fun.

A great newscast is *thought-provoking* by nature of its perspective and balance. Most people have a single point of view. Balanced stories, on the other hand, have several points of view, and if presented in a compelling, responsible and informative way, will teach those consuming the newscast.

It is *empowering* because it offers solutions and motivates consumers of the newscast to take action, to take matters into their own hands. People can learn how to get refunds, how to ask for a raise, how to find a better job or how to get rid of a neighborhood nuisance.

It is *disconcerting* because its reflection of events is sometimes a reality check. Bad things happen to good people. There is such a thing as "evil" and sometimes there is no justice. Consumers of a great newscast are not naïve by the time they've finished watching the show; they're aware and possibly ready to take action to keep themselves and their loved ones safe.

At the end of the day, the great newscast is *comfortable* because it's been perfectly executed with a great deal of attention to detail. It is glitch-free and technically clean. Video is allowed to shine. Sound is crisp. Storytelling is memorable. The roller coaster ride has moved perfectly uphill and downhill, and has been an exhilarating experience that makes the consumers want to come back and get in line again. And it's all been presented by a team of professional, approachable people, with chemistry that draws the consumer into the family.

Deliver What You Promise

Television and radio stations get carried away with teases. The object, of course, is to lure the audience into watching or listening. During sweep months in television, creative advertising can and often does mislead viewers as to what is actually being presented.

Here's a promo:

It's the diet everyone's been waiting for. Some people are call-
ing it a miracle. Pounds fall away while you sleep. Tonight at eleven
we'll show you what this new diet is and how it works. Get ready to
lose weight with News Channel 1 at eleven.

Here's the story:

Some people are calling it a miracle—lose weight while you
sleep—so News Channel 1 investigated to find out what this revolu-
tionary new diet is all about. It's called "Sleep Away." The makers of
the diet supplement are advertising that just two spoonfuls of this liq-
uid will take the inches off while you sleep, but there's a catch. You
can't eat anything for four hour before you take this potion and can
have no-middle-of-the-night snacks. The instructions also say you
must exercise for at least twenty minutes every day.

The story goes on to feature a doctor who explains that by exercising and changing your eating habits you would lose weight even
without this new diet formula.

Viewers tune in thinking they are going to get information
about a new miracle drug that will allow them to lose weight while
they sleep, when in fact they hear just the opposite. The viewers are
disappointed in the report; the station get complaints that it has mis-
led the viewers with the promotion and some people may go elsewhere for their news. If you're in a rating period, even if they tune to
another station for just a few days, it could hurt.

Here's a better way the promo could have been handled.

It's being advertised as the new miracle diet. You lose pounds
and inches as you sleep. Too good to be true? News Channel 1 put
Sleep Away to the test. We put two groups of people on this diet with
different instructions. You will be surprised to see what happened and
why. It's a News Channel 1 exclusive, tonight at eleven.

Here you are not promising a story you are not going to deliver. In fact, you are creating intrigue and turning false hope into an
investigation.

During the February rating period in 2001, a Pittsburgh television station ran a promotional spot with an announcer who stated,
"Our Consumer Watch reporter takes action for you by exposing
X-rated cartoons being rented to kids." But in the piece, the reporter
made clear the videos were unrated, not X-rated, and she began by
saying, "We're not talking about hard-core pornography here."

Here's how these misleading promotions usually get on the air. A sweeps meeting is held in the newsroom. Everyone pitches ideas and the managers pick the best ones. The stories are conveyed to the promotion department and then an on-air promotion campaign is created. Overzealous promotion writers trying to get ratings can step over the line and turn news stories into circus acts. Regrettably, it happens all the time.

Oftentimes the news managers never see the promotion before it airs and by that time it's too late; the damage has been done.

Other times, the promotion and story start out on the same page, but as the reporter gets into his or her story its focus changes. No one notifies the promotion department and the on-air promotion and the story go off in two separate directions.

I can't stress enough how important it is for the journalist to keep management informed every step of the way through the reporting of a story that you know is going to be promoted. This is being a responsible journalist; it will also keep you out of trouble with your boss.

Overzealous promo writers, or news managers who don't accurately communicate what the story actually is, are irresponsible. The audience can only take so many deceptions before the station's reputation is tarnished and viewers or listeners will go elsewhere for the news. The moral to the story: Don't mislead the audience. Deliver what you promise.

Broadcasting Business

With the advent of CNBC, CNN-FN and others, business reporting has reached a new pinnacle. Even so, broadcasting business reports can be very tricky business. Page Hopkins, an anchor and reporter for Bloomberg Television who delivers business news on three different networks across the nation every day, writes:

When it comes to financial news, ethics can be a minefield. You always have to be extra cautious that you don't characterize any company news as bad or good since what you are saying could move the markets. In general news, you can say, "We have a sad story to tell you about a seeing eye dog was run over while rescuing his owner..."; of course, everyone would agree that this is sad news. In financial news, what may seem universally regarded as bad news, such as weak earnings, cannot be characterized *any* particular way. You can only say, "Company X reported earnings this morning, missing street estimates by a nickel." You cannot say "Bad news out of company X today as their earnings miss the street." You have to let the investors come to that conclusion.

Interviews are another area where the anchor has to beware. Many analysts are lauding stocks for reasons you may not be aware of and you have to be on them to explain why they have a "buy" on a certain company versus a competitor. Several analysts are so powerful that whatever they tell you will move the stock within moments and they know it, so you have to be vigilant when interviewing them.

Of all types of news, financial news must be the most unbiased. You cannot let emotions trickle into the content at all. You have to stand guard at the portal of facts. You have to be completely prepared when doing interviews, to make sure you don't let a guest come on set and push the stocks he's long in. It's the same set of ethics you bring to general news, only your accountability is constantly being checked.

Responsible Radio Journalism

Many of us forget that, before this age of instant pictures and excitable television reporters, there was radio.

On December 24, 1906, Reginald Fessenden, an electrical engineering professor at the University of Pittsburgh, applied what he called the continuous wave theory. In a shore telegraph station in Brant Rock, Massachusetts, Fessenden successfully transmitted a radio wave to a receiver that reproduced the original sound. He transmitted Bible and poetry readings. This event was marked as the first radio broadcast, and ushered in the age of broadcast messaging.

By the mid-1920s, radio stations were receiving licenses all over the country. Today, radio has taken on new complexities and is broadcast both through conventional transmitters and over the Internet.

Mike Freedman has been a broadcaster for over 30 years. Prior to becoming vice president and professional lecturer in broadcast journalism at George Washington University, Mike was the president of

CBS Radio News, where he won multiple awards including seven Murrow Awards. He offers the following advice for radio journalists:

Radio is the most intimate of all media, representing the classic form of electronic one-to-one communication. People wake up to it, shower with it, drive to and from work with it, run with it and go to sleep with it. Radio's portability and dependability have earned it a special place in American life. It has become as second nature to us as combing our hair and brushing our teeth.

It has also become something people do when they're doing something else!

The best radio news broadcasters understand this and play to their audience. CBS (Radio) News Capitol Hill correspondent Bob Fuss, for instance, always writes simply and conversationally. He only uses words that people will know because, unlike newspaper readers, radio listeners cannot go back and hear it again.

In commercial radio today, success equals excellent writing, superior use of sound and the ability to tell a good story—in 25 seconds or less! Anchors and reporters know you can't afford to waste a single word.

So how do you keep it simple without underestimating the intelligence of your audience? How do you write a substantive story in 25 seconds? How do you keep the attention of the listener while competing with traffic or the shaver? In short, how can you be a responsible radio journalist in this day and age?

First, you have to subscribe to the belief that even though times change, good journalism doesn't. Those managing and working in solid newsrooms gather, sort and report—in that order. I don't know of anyone who would recommend putting immediacy before accuracy. Yet, stations and networks are getting tripped up with greater frequency for doing just that. In the end, there is no reward for being first and being wrong.

Second, know the news. Read at least one major newspaper every day. Even if a piece you write is 25 seconds long, you need to know the whole story in order to write it well.

George Avakain, Mike Freedman, Tony Bennett and Dick Golden during radio taping—Courtesy Mike Freedman

That said, the best radio newscasts are compelling, timely and cohesive. They keep you riveted from beginning to end. A live, remote open from the scene of a story lends a dramatic touch. It also lets the listener know you are there.

Use of relevant natural sound like a thunderstorm or a mass of people add dimension to a radio story. In addition, the ROSR, a Radio On Scene Report in which the correspondent records a description of a dramatic situation with all of the natural sound in the background, takes the listener right onto the convention floor hall or into the streets.

Whip-arounds can be very dynamic. During a recent hurricane, CBS Radio News correspondents and stringers lined the East Coast from Florida to Maryland. The first correspondent opened the newscast and within 60 seconds, a total of four live reports aired with each person handing off to the next in a descriptive manner. ("Now let's move 60 miles up the coast to the Outer Banks of North Carolina where my colleague…is standing by.")

An anchor engaging in a question and answer conversation with a correspondent in the field can also be very effective. It's amazing how much information can be conveyed in 25 seconds if everyone is literally on the same page.

Words that convey immediacy can make a big difference in a newscast. When an anchor says that a story has broken "within the past hour" or rescue efforts are "about to get underway," listeners believe they are getting the very latest news.

Finally, in today's radio world, "relatability" rules. This applies to the broadcast voice as well as story selection and use of sound and writing. George Washington University journalism professor Al May, a former political writer for the *Atlanta Journal-Constitution*, tells aspiring reporters that, in addition to finding out who, what, where, when, why and how, you also have to answer the question, "So what?"

That's the relatability factor.

Radio news is a tough business today. The universe is shrinking, competitive pressures are enormous and in many cases, salaries don't compare with those in television. Yet, the medium that invented broadcast journalism survives and thrives today because of its uncanny ability to reinvent itself and the dedication of those who strive to make it relevant.

Honey, We Shrunk the Audience

Radio news ratings are remaining relatively stable while television ratings are shrinking at an alarming rate. In the early days of television, viewers had to get up from the couch or bed and walk over to the TV to change the channel. Today every TV is sold with a remote control, and thus enter the couch surfers. In addition, the number of different channels available on cable and satellite is growing, and the audience is now being divided among all these channels. Although local news remains the only source for a community's news, weather and sports in a single program, the audience is not watching as much news as they used to, and they're watching in fewer numbers. Countless studies speculate as to why news ratings both locally and nationally are on the decline. Audience fragmentation, loss of interest, audience composition change, and other information and entertainment sources (like the Internet) are drawing the viewers away.

Courtesy Mike Luckovich and Creators Syndicate, Inc.

In today's demanding environment we have to be smarter and produce a better product; the days of reveling in being the number one station or settling for second place are gone. Most number one stations have remained in first place but at the cost of lower overall ratings, which affect sales and the station's bottom line.

In January of 2001 cutbacks were the name of the game. Hundreds of journalists and technicians were laid off, forced into early retirement or fired. It all seemed to happen in very short period of time.

On January 11, 2001, *Variety* reported:

With the ad sales marketplace continuing to head south, NBC is expected to lay off as many as 600 employees over the next six months as part of a network-wide cost-cutting initiative.

Pink slips could start flying within the next few weeks, as NBC seeks to trim between 5% and 10% of its workforce of 6,000. Cuts are expected across the board in every department and every division of NBC Inc.—including entertainment and news, as well as cable channels MSNBC, CNBC and the NBC-owned stations.

On January 18, 2001, the *Atlanta Journal-Constitution* reported:

> Four hundred CNN workers will lose their jobs. And employees who remain will be called on to do more: Feed news to all of CNN's 34 TV networks, Web sites and radio networks, rather than specializing in one medium.

In addition, News Corp. (FOX) and ABC initiated hiring freezes or other job-cutting measures.

With thousands of journalism jobs being cut in early 2001, many journalists were looking for work. Times appeared bleak. But the best and most responsible journalists with solid reputations landed on their feet and found suitable new jobs.

CHAPTER 5

Responsible Print Journalism

You're only as good as your last story.

Helen Thomas

In the Beginning...

From the time of the first printed newspapers, questions were raised about the validity of stories and their sources. The first regularly published paper in America was said to be the *Boston News-Letter,* first published on April 24, 1704. The paper reported news from London and many of the printed items had no attributed source. Newspapers were the primary source of information, however, and as time passed they began to be held to tougher standards.

Although investigative journalism likely was practiced by the very first reporters, it gained new notoriety in 1871. A famous African explorer was missing and the *New York Herald* sent a young reporter, Henry M. Stanley, to find him. For two years the paper printed stories of Stanley's search and public interest grew with each printed page. Stanley's account of scene that took place three hundred yards from the village of Ujiji took journalism to a new level:

The crowds are dense about me. Suddenly I hear a voice on my right say,—

Henry Stanley—Courtesy New York Herald *Archive*

"Good morning, sir!"

Startled at hearing this greeting in the midst of such a crowd of black people, I turn sharply around in search of the man, and see him at my side, with the blackest of faces, but animated and joyous—a man dressed in a long white shirt, with a turban of American sheeting around his woolly head, and I ask:—

"Who the mischief are you?"

"I am Susi, the servant of Dr. Livingstone," said he, smiling and showing a gleaming row of teeth.

"What! Is Dr. Livingstone here?"

"Yes, sir."

"In this village?"

"Yes, sir."

"Are you sure?"

"Sure, sure, sir. Why, I leave him just now."

"Good morning, sir," said another voice.

"Hallo," said I, "is this another one?"

"Yes, sir."

"Well, what is your name?"

"My name is Chumah, sir."

"What! are you Chumah, the friend of Wekotani?"

"Yes, sir."

"And is the Doctor well?"

"Not very well, sir."

"Where has he been so long?"

"In Manyuema."

"Now, you, Susi, run, and tell the Doctor I am coming."

"Yes, sir," and off he darted like a madman.

But by this time we were within two hundred yards of the village, and the multitude was getting denser, and almost preventing our march. Flags and streamers were out; Arabs and Wangwana were pushing their way through the natives in order to greet us, for, according to their account, we belonged to them. But the great wonder of all was, "How did you come from Unyanyembe?"

Soon Susi came running back, and asked me my name; he had told the Doctor that I was coming, but the Doctor was too surprised to believe him, and, when the Doctor asked him my name, Susi was rather staggered. But, during Susi's absence, the news had been conveyed to the Doctor that it was surely a white man that was coming, whose guns were firing and whose flag could be seen; and the great Arab magnates of Ujiji—Mohammed bin Sali, Sayd bin Majid, Abid bin Suliman, Mohammed bin Gharib, and others—had gathered together before the Doctor's house, and the Doctor had come out from his veranda to discuss the matter and await my arrival.

In the meantime, the head of the expedition had halted, and the kirangozi was out of the ranks, holding his flag aloft, and Selim said to me, "I see the Doctor, sir. Oh, what an old man! He has got a white beard." And I—what would I not have given for a bit of friendly wilderness, where, unseen, I might vent my joy in some mad freak, such as idiotically biting my hand, turning somersaults, or slashing at trees, in order to allay those exciting feelings that were well-nigh uncontrollable. My heart beats fast, but I must not let my face betray my emotions, lest it shall detract from the dignity of a white man appearing under such extraordinary circumstances.

So I did that which I thought was most dignified. I pushed back the crowds, and, passing from the rear, walked down a living avenue of people until I came in front of the semicircle of Arabs, in the front of which stood the white man with the grey beard. As I advanced slowly towards him, I noticed he was pale, looked wearied, had a grey beard, wore a bluish cap with a faded gold band round it, had on a red-sleeved waistcoat and a pair of grey tweed trousers. I would have run to him, only I was a coward in the presence of such a mob—would have embraced him, only he being an Englishman, I did not know how he would receive me; so I did what cowardice and false pride suggested was the best thing—walked deliberately to him, took off my hat, and said:—

"Dr. Livingstone, I presume?"

"Yes," said he, with a kind smile, lifting his cap slightly.

I replace my hat on my head, and he puts on his cap, and we both grasp hands, and I then say aloud:

—"I thank God, Doctor, I have been permitted to see you." He answered, "I feel thankful that I am here to welcome you."

The phrase "Doctor Livingstone, I presume" became widely used and Stanley's diaries were the subject of numerous books—and, later, movies. Even though Henry Stanley's reporting showed a remarkable quest for the sake of investigative journalism, lessons can also be learned from the circumstances under which he was given the assignment. When Stanley was assigned to the story, the publisher of the paper, by Stanley's own account, ordered him to "Take what you want, but find Livingstone." In today's newsroom climate, some editors still make "or else" demands on their reporters. But unlike in Stanley's time, today, most journalists ask, "Or what?" calling the bluff. Henry Stanley set out on a dangerous journey not knowing if he'd ever come back. Today, when a reporter leaves a newsroom there's no such uncertainty.

Investigative news assignments can be tricky, and when executed well, reap rewards. But unlike Stanley, it's best to talk over assignments with others, get second opinions and think story execution through. When stories are discussed among two or more people before they are printed, good results usually ensue.

Underpaid, Overworked and Always under a Deadline

The good news now is that newspapers, magazines and the Internet give responsible journalists plenty of space to tell the story, time to develop it and headlines to promote it. The bad news is that when a mistake is made or misinformation is printed, readers have plenty of time to find it. In broadcasting, a story goes by in seconds, and unless viewers or listeners pay close attention, they may not catch an error. Print media has to go the extra mile and pay special attention to detail.

Newspaper and magazine reporting must apply a different standard from broadcast reporting. Even the positioning of information within the body of the text can cause misunderstanding. When an article is divided among more than one page, many readers only read the first part. If a newspaper presents one side of a controversial issue on the first page of an article, and the opposite point of view on an inside page, the reader could interpret this as bias.

Using what I call the *progressive writing style* is a good tool for print journalists. Begin your story with both sides of the issue. Progress to the story background or explanation, then present the different angles, keeping your column space in mind. Easier said than done, but a good rule of thumb. As Jack Fuller, president of Tribune

Publishing, puts it, "When I was a reporter, I tried to apply a kind of golden rule: to state the opposite point of view as forcefully as I would have someone state mine."

It also helps to find out how your story is going to be composed. This is especially important when presenting a complex story with passionate arguments. A good print story should be a complete package. It should have an impressive picture, compelling copy, and a strong headline.

Headlines are usually written by someone other than the reporter; thus, it's important for the headline writer to read the entire story. You'd be surprised how many times this doesn't happen, and there are even occasions where the headline is written before the story. One of satirist Will Rogers' favorite remarks was, "All I know is what I read in the paper." He often commented on the headlines he saw, some of which made perfect copy for his humorous speeches. Here are just a few:

> Include Your Children When Baking Cookies
> Enraged Cow Injures Farmer with Ax
> Deer Kill 17,000
> Kids Make Nutritious Snacks
> Red Tape Holds Up New Bridge
> Stolen Painting Found by Tree
> Queen Mary Having Bottom Scraped
> Grandmother of Eight Makes Hole in One
> House Passes Gas Tax onto Senate

You have to wonder just how these headlines ended up being printed in respectable papers.

John Galsworthy wrote, "headlines are twice the size of the events." The "above the fold" headline you see as you walk by a newspaper vending machine or when you first unwrap the morning paper is there to pique your curiosity, to make you read the story. Curiosity is one reason people pick up a newspaper or turn on a news broadcast. Jack Fuller characterizes curiosity as being partly responsible for a fundamental change in our industry:

> When I was starting in the newspaper business, people were deeply involved in the minutia of local politics. Today, if I were to stand up in the newsroom at the *Chicago Tribune*

and shout out the question, "How many of you can tell me the name of your state representative?" I wouldn't see a whole bunch of hands and mine probably wouldn't be among them. There's been a big change in the areas that people are curious about. You've seen news which actually responds to human curiosity. That's what defines news, and news has to shift along with it. This causes people to be nervous because they think that news should lead curiosity, which it should, but there are limits to the extent to which it can.

The Internet: Where Print Meets Broadcasting

The Internet has changed our lives in many ways. In the years to come, we will see the convergence of television and the Internet into one family entertainment unit on a much broader scale than what services like Web-TV offer us now.

Sam Donaldson of ABC News is a pioneer in the field of "Web-casting" news via the Internet. He is standing on the bridge between broadcasting and the Internet.

One of the big questions journalists are asking today is: what role will the Internet ultimately play in the dissemination of news?

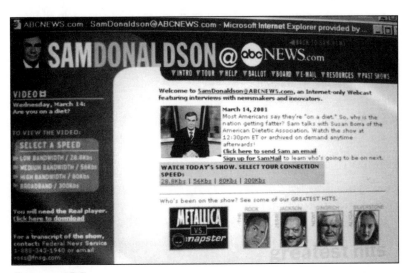

Courtesy ABC

Will there eventually be a convergence of broadcast, newspapers and the Internet?

Donaldson thinks there are two answers to this question:

First, at the moment people are increasingly coming to the Internet to get their news. At this point it's mainly text; they get the news by reading. There are short streaming video clips that some Web sites provide. 30 seconds of a hurricane or someone speaking. In April of 2000 my show is still the only regularly scheduled Internet news broadcast.

But secondly, down the line, the communications belt for all communications will be the Internet. I think that some day there will be a screen in people's homes in various rooms and they can sit down in front of that screen and do whatever they want. They can check their stocks, watch *Monday Night Football* or look up something in the encyclopedia or even buy cheap airline tickets. What I'm saying is, I think that all of what is now television and radio, not just printed media, will come into your home or business over the Internet. It's going to be almost indistinguishable to say, "We watch WJLA-TV in Washington for a program." You may watch WJLA's Web site to watch *Who Wants to Be a Millionaire*. When I say this our ABC affiliate relations people are driven up the wall. I don't blame them.

People say to me, "With hundreds of thousands of Web sites, what about the quality?" If they come onto a Web site and it says TWA 800 was shot down by a missile from a Navy submarine, how are they to know it's a bunch of hogwash? Eventually people will gravitate to the respected newsgathering sites and I trust ABC will be one of them. People know, just as today they know what broadcast news organizations they can trust. The untrustworthy Web sites just won't have many visitors.

I don't feel any additional responsibility that I wouldn't feel reporting for the television network. All of the things a responsible journalist should do in the way of checking stories, checking facts and preparing material for an audience are the same. The Internet, however, does allow a certain kind of looseness that I think we don't have in commercial broadcasting. I feel free to show people a different side of my personality in the sense that I tease people sometimes, I talk in different terms. We're still careful not to use vulgarity, or to disparage people's national origin, color, creed or any of that. So I'm not talking about "Shock Jock" work.

The Internet is a different presentation. It's almost like radio. Unlike a television program, radio is an intimate form of communication. The audience forms a bond, if you're lucky. I sense that the audience I'm taking to rather likes the fact that I'm myself, rather than it being very structured and using words that I would want on my tombstone.

Correction!

The Internet provides a new challenge to responsible print journalism. Now that many newspapers are available on the Web, newspapers must take greater care to correct errors, to ensure that they do not live on in Internet archives.

This article on the difficulty of Web site corrections originally appeared online in the February 8, 1999, edition of *Editor & Publisher*. The author, Frank Sennett, is a features editor at MTVi and co-creator of the alternative-press portal *Newcity.com*. Frank urges his colleagues to admit mistakes more openly. He writes:

On Jan. 16, 1999, The Associated Press ran this story about alleged human-rights abuses in Mexico. The Jan. 14 story, based on a report by the organization Human Rights Watch, "said that Mexican judges, prosecutors and law-enforcement officers collude to torture suspects, illegally obtain evidence and block investigations into human rights violations," the correction read. However, the AP continued, "The report by Human Rights Watch did not say that judges collude in those acts. The group said that by failing to question evidence obtained through torture, judges become complicit in the abuse."

That's the kind of mistake that causes editors to lose their breath and media lawyers to lose sleep. But a Jan. 27 Web search found uncorrected copies of the story littering the archives of several online news organizations more than 10 days after the AP sent out its alert. The Las Vegas Sun still offered readers the Mexico mistake, as did ABC News.com and Yahoo! News. (Although a link to the correction popped up in the Yahoo! search, the original story file ran uncorrected). The version in the St. Louis Post-Dispatch archives even included the collusion allegation in its headline.

Rather than an isolated incident, this proliferation of an info landmine is indicative of a deep-seated problem news providers face in dealing with corrections on the Web. Newsies who fail to acknowledge their errors risk losing credibility with consumers. Without the polish of prominent corrections, inaccurate rough drafts of history darken the media's already tarnished image. But as the news cycle continues to speed up, Internet info providers—newspaper, magazine, and broadcast sites, as well as Web-only publications—are falling behind in their efforts to come clean with an increasingly fed-up public.

The good news is that most people don't expect news organizations to be perfect; they simply insist reporters and editors admit when they stumble. That's what the American Society of Newspaper Editors found recently when it surveyed 3,000 Americans and 16 focus groups on the issue of media credibility.

Of those polled, only 19% reported "always" seeing a correction after spotting a mistake in their daily paper; 40% said they "sometimes" see one; 22% find them "rarely"; and 11% "never" see corrections (8% didn't know if they've seen any). However, 63% of respondents contend that seeing corrections makes them "feel better...about the quality of news coverage."

The message to news organizations, summed up by one focus-group participant, is simple: "If there's a mistake, admit it. People are more likely to believe you. Don't hide it in small print. Let them know you want them to know your mistakes."

The Correct Path

Let's assume Internet news providers want to admit and rectify their errors. Why, then, is it so difficult to find corrections on most sites? One problem is that the Web is still in its infancy as a popular medium for news, so industry-wide content standards are few.

Another is that the owners of many online media outlets are not used to running corrections on a regular basis: broadcasters rarely devote precious airtime to admitting mistakes and independent site operators may have no journalism training. Newspaper and magazine sites may simply not find enough homepage space to add standing corrections links.

But as the American Society of Newspaper Editors concluded, "Admitting errors and running corrections helps, not hurts, credibility." So not only is fessing up to mistakes the ethical thing to do, it can even bolster a news site's reputation—and, ultimately, its bottom line. Which means it's high time for online info providers to adopt new standards for publishing corrections on their sites.

For the Record

Every news site should provide readers with a prominent link to its corrections page. That link might be a standing one—always present in the same spot on the homepage or in the table of contents—making the corrections section easier for readers to find and Webmasters to update. For instance, The Washington Post runs a "Correction" header at the very top of its "Front Section" story scroll.

Or the link might float throughout the site, landing in the section where the error first appeared. That's what Baltimore's The Sun does at sunspot.net. In fact, the Baltimore site takes an exemplary approach to fixing its mistakes. For instance, it specifically notes the original error in the correction. "The name of the company is Autopay Data Processing Services Inc., not Accupay," a recent correction said. Most papers simply would leave readers in the dark by writing, "Autopay Data Processing Services Inc. was misidentified." And each item ends with the line; "The Sun regrets the error."

But as the president is so fond of saying, "We can do better." For example, the Chicago Tribune includes corrections at the bottom of archived stories that contain factual errors. If that seems to make for a jarring reader experience, updating the text in the main story file and providing a link to the correction would seem to be a satisfactory compromise. But because The Sun's correction cited above was not present in the archived version of the story, that mistake will live on. To work effectively, the correction process must be a two-step one in which news sites prominently acknowledge mistakes when they are discovered, and then append the original story file with a note updating the material. This is a better approach than simply erasing errors from a story file, which smacks of a mistake-hiding rewrite of history.

It's also important to make readers feel involved in the correction process. Reader representatives and ombudsmen are great, but most news organizations don't feel they can afford to hire them. But there's a simple, inexpensive way to invite readers to keep info sites on their toes: include an editor's contact info in every correction file. "The Examiner corrects errors," reads the correction page at sfgate.com. "Please notify the editor: P.O. Box 7260, San Francisco 94120." That's great, but an e-mail link would be even more helpful.

The San Francisco Chronicle, which shares the sfgate .com site as part of a joint operating agreement, doesn't provide contact info in its corrections section, but it does eliminate the passive voice, telling readers exactly where the breakdown took place. "Because of an editing error, the number of employees laid off by Franklin Resources was misstated," a recent item began. "In an item that appeared in the Business section yesterday, Reuters news service incorrectly stated Inktomi Corp.'s first-quarter loss," started another sfgate.com correction.

What it all adds up to is a commitment by media outlets to show readers they are honorable enough to admit their mistakes, and that they take them as seriously as the problems they uncover in the outside world. Any news site that doesn't correct its factual slipups in a similar fashion is making a grave error.

If you want to track newspaper mistakes and read more, just click on *slipup.com*.

Checking Your Research Skills

When you're working in the print arena, time is on your side. If you have the time to research, you have time to make a better more interesting story. More than any other type of journalist, a print reporter can benefit from honing his or her research skills.

Bill Dedman won the Pulitzer Prize for Investigative Reporting for a story he wrote for the *Atlanta Journal-Constitution* on discrimination by lenders. He devoted himself to helping other journalists be the best they can be, and he has taken the time to come up with ideas for responsible research. His Web site, *Powerreporting.com*, offers good tools for all journalists, not just those in print media. Here are nine questions he has come up with to make you think and do your homework. As an exercise in journalistic research, try hitting the books and searching the Internet to see if you can find the answers. If you have a tough time, visit *Powerreporting.com* and click on "Treasure Hunt." You'll see these same questions (plus a few more), but you'll also find how he did the actual research.

1. Adjust for inflation. You're editing an article that refers to Babe Ruth's salary of $80,000 in 1931 (when, as he said, he "had a better year" than President Hoover). How much would that be in today's dollars?

2. Check your law. A 9-year-old girl has been killed riding her bike. She was not wearing a helmet. What is your state or city law on bicycle helmets?

3. Prep for an interview. In 10 minutes you'll be covering a speech by an author named Grossman, who contends that video games are a cause of school shootings, because they condition children to kill. But you have an early deadline, so you have to do the interview before the speech. The book has "killing" in the title. What is the exact title? What term did he coin? What other books has he written? What town is he from, and why might that be interesting? What questions do you want to ask him before the speech?

4. Source a quotation. When the nominees for president pick women as running mates, we'll have to be careful with that saying, "politics makes strange bedfellows." Who coined that maxim? And isn't there an earlier use of the phrase, "strange bedfellows"? Who said it first?

5. Background a business executive. Melvin J. Gordon just gave a huge contribution to your art museum. All you know is that he runs a company in the U.S. Who is he? What company? Besides its namesake product, what else does this company produce? What is his annual salary? What was his total cash compensation? How much is he worth (at least in company stock), as of today?

6. Find an unnamed person. AP is reporting the first ID of a victim of the Amtrak train crash near Bourbonnais, Ill. There's no name, but she was a grandmother and owned a bed and breakfast in Nesbit, Miss. What is the name and phone number of the B&B? Without calling the B&B, find her name.

7. Background a Web site. Matt Drudge has some gossip about your editor on his Web site, at *http://www.drudgereport.com.* You need to reach Drudge by phone. All you know is his Web site address. From that, find his phone number. (It's not on his site.)

8. Spot a trend. It's bridal story time. What has happened to the age at which people get married for the first time, over the past 100 years, in the U.S.? (Hint: Not quite what you think.)

9. See where you rank. Estimates of poverty in every school district in the U.S. are made every few years by the U.S. Census Bureau. You can find this file on the Census site, How does your school district rank, among those in your state, in percentage of children in poverty?

Answers

1. Ruth's $80,000 in 1931 would be worth about $931,000, as of May 2001.

2. A good list of state and city laws on bicycle helmets is at the Bicycle Helmet Safety Institute [*www.helmets.org/webdocs/mandator.htm*]. This link is available from its main page. The institute explains, "There is no federal law in the U.S. requiring helmets. States and localities began adopting laws in 1987, but there is no formal central registry for them."

3. Grossman's book is called "On Killing: The Psychological Cost of Learning to Kill in War and Society." He claims to have coined the term, "killology." He has a newer book, "Stop Teaching Our Kids to Kill: A Call to Action Against TV, Movie and Video Game Violence." He lives in Jonesboro, Ark., site of a shooting at Westside Middle School.

The questions are up to you.... [See the Web site for examples.]

4. This one comes from a newspaperman or Shakespeare, depending on your point of view. Quotations on the Web can be maddening, because of the many variations and uncertain sourcing. (If you believe the Web, Mark Twain said everything except part of what's in the Bible.)

Yes, "politics makes strange bedfellows," but the phrase is much older. The earliest reference seems to come from Shakespeare. Trinculo, a jester, says in the "The Tempest," "Misery acquaints a man with strange bedfellows." (Act 2, Scene 2)

The politics maxim seems to be correctly ascribed to Charles Dudley Warner, a Connecticut newspaperman. Warner was also a neighbor of Mark Twain, and his collaborator on "The Gilded Age." Many of Warner's best lines are falsely attributed to Twain, including "Everybody talks about the weather, but no one does anything about it."

5. Melvin J. Gordon is the chairman of the board, president and chief executive officer of Tootsie Roll Industries Inc., the candy company in Chicago. It makes Tootsie Rolls, Junior Mints, Mason Dots, and Sugar Daddy.

The latest company filing is now nearly one year old, but his salary in 1998 was $955,000, and his total cash compensation was $1,885,000, counting a bonus of $930,000. He owned a smidge more than one million shares of stock, and his wife owned 6.5 million shares. Each share of stock is worth about $30, so that makes their paper net worth, in stock, about $225 million.

6. The bed and breakfast in Nesbit, Miss., is the Bonne Terre County Inn and Cafe. When you find the phone number you'll also learn the innkeepers were Max and June Bonnin. Mrs. Bonnin was known as a cancer survivor, who beat Hodgkin's without radiation or chemotherapy.

7. [We can't publish the number, but here's a clue to see if you've got the right answer—the last four digits contain two 2's, a "0" and a "1".]

8. The median age of first marriage has gone up—but it hasn't gone up uniformly. First it went down, then up. We remember that people used to get married younger. My grandmother remembered that people used to get married older.

9. The 20 largest school districts vary widely in poverty, from about half the students in Detroit to less than 10 percent in three districts surrounding Washington, D.C. The list: Detroit, 48%; Houston, 41%; NYC, 39%; Los Angeles, 39%; Philadelphia, 36%; Chicago, 35%; Dallas, 34%; Dade County (Miami), Fla., 32%; Memphis, 32%; San Diego, 27%; Hillsborough County, Fla., 22%; Duval County, Fla., 20%; Broward County, Fla., 17%; Orange County, Fla., 17%; Palm Beach County, Fla., 17%; Clark County, Nev., etc.

CHAPTER 6

Look Responsible

Good clothes open all doors.

Thomas Fuller

Every time you step before a television camera, you're being judged. Whether they realize it or not, television viewers make instant evaluations based on the way a journalist presents him- or herself. That judgmental attitude puts your credibility on the line before you even speak one word.

Following are important tips to help your on-air presentation.

Dress Responsibly

A good primer for everyone is the book *Dress for Success*. For male television reporters, a nicely tailored suit or sport jacket is the general rule. Never wear jeans unless it's for effect or because you're in rugged surroundings. For women, a business suit or dress is the order of the day. Be careful not to show too much leg—or anything else, for that matter. Be mindful of hemlines, especially while conducting a sit-down interview. Female reporters should take care not to wear revealing or low-cut dresses while reporting from black-tie events. This is not appropriate for local news reporting.

Courtesy KDNL-TV

The primary rules are, don't wear anything that's distracting, be fashionable but conservative, and wear clothes that are in "good taste."

As a news director, one of my pet peeves is journalists wearing hats on the air. Many reporters like to wear hats, but I prefer they don't. Here's why:

Hats tend to cut off half your face. Television cameras shoot for the best available light. When a hat creates a shadow, the camera will make the upper part of your face dark if not black. This is a problem because the viewer wants to see your eyes. We are all taught from the very first day in the business that eye contact is one of the most important factors for on-air reporting. Hats also tend to distract from your on-camera presence. The viewer will tend to look at your hat instead of listening to what you are saying.

If you can, take your hat off just before you go on the air. Make an exception only to protect yourself in very cold temperatures or other bad weather conditions, or if the hat is part of your story.

The Makeup Dilemma: How Much Is Too Much?

As a woman, the worst thing that can happen to you is to be compared to Tammy Faye Baker or Katherine Harris. As a man, you don't want to look like you're ready to go out trick or treating.

Common complaints from the news director:

* Your lipstick is too dark (or bright).
* You have too much eye shadow on.
* Your cheeks are too rosy; you're wearing too much blush.

As veteran broadcasters know, the camera can play tricks on you. What you see in the mirror when you put your makeup on may not be what the camera sees. The best way to try out new makeup is to do a simple camera test. Put your makeup on, head into the studio and have them make a quick tape of you on each of the cameras. Then look and see how the studio lighting has affected your appearance. If you are unsure if you look just right, ask a news manager. The managers want you to look your best, so they'll be honest.

Dana Adam's Makeup Tips

Dana Adams worked as an NBC network correspondent and an evening news anchor in both Los Angeles and New York City. She's now a talent and makeup coach for stations across the county.

Broadcasters may think what they say is a lot more important than how they look. To a certain extent, that is true.

Dana Adams at WCBS-TV—Courtesy Dana Adams

However, if a broadcaster's appearance is distracting, then the viewers won't hear a word that is said. Therefore, like it or not, makeup is a very important aspect of a newscaster's appearance.

The best makeup is makeup that is not noticed. If the mention of a broadcaster's name conjures up comments about that person's makeup, than he or she is doing something wrong. Makeup should accentuate a person's good features and hide the bad ones. You don't want to notice things like eye shadow, liner and blush. You do want to notice the color and shape of a person's eyes and face.

Applying makeup for television is much more difficult than putting it on for real-life situations. In person, a face is three-dimensional. On television, it appears two-dimensional, which makes the face look flat and wide. This effect, coupled with unflattering shadows that the harsh lights often cast, can make the best-looking person look terrible on camera. Therefore, makeup must be used to bring out features like jaw lines and cheekbones, and to compensate for dark shadows created by the lighting.

A basic rule of thumb for newscasters: find a look that you like and stick with it. Nothing is more distracting than on-air talent who change their appearance every week. Women are notorious for this when it comes to hair. We all have bad hair days. But changing the cut and color on a regular basis is distracting for the viewer. The same applies to makeup. It's all right to vary your lipstick color to a certain extent, but your overall look should be consistent from day to day.

What does vary when it comes to makeup is how much to put on. Reporting dayside in the field requires the least amount of makeup because you are most often dealing with natural light. Reporting nightside in the field requires a little more makeup, because most often you are artificially lit in front of a darker background. Anchoring or reporting in the studio requires the most makeup because of the harshness of the lights. You don't have to change the colors you use, just the degree of application. Therefore, during the day, your makeup should look close to how it would appear if you were not on television. In fact, men shouldn't need anything more than a little translucent powder to cut shininess. At night, the application should be slightly heavier for women. Men, however, can still get away with just powder. For studio lighting, men need to apply makeup they wouldn't normally wear in the field, which will be discussed later in this chapter. Women need to apply the same makeup, just more of it.

Before discussing makeup specifically for women and men, I want to share one trick of the trade that can be helpful to any tired newscaster after a late night. The best way to get rid of those unsightly bags under the eyes is to use Preparation H. It's always difficult to get people to put hemorrhoid cream on their face, but anyone who has tried this becomes a believer. The reason it works is simple. Preparation H shrinks swollen tissue. The tissue under your eyes is as delicate as the tissue around the area the cream is normally applied. Therefore it is as effective at reducing the swelling under your eyes as it is down under!

Makeup for Women

Base Makeup:

Step one: moisturizer. Always moisturize your face and neck before applying makeup. The smoother your face, the better the base makeup will go on. Also, avoid sunburns and peeling, because even the most skilled makeup artist can't hide flaking skin.

Step two: concealer and foundation. When choosing these items, it's best to buy brands made specifically for film and television use. A beauty supply store will have this type of selection. MAC Makeup also has a line of studio makeup.

Your concealer should be lighter than your foundation, but not chalk white. Use concealer under the eyes to hide circles, and anywhere else you want to hide something. Scars, blemishes, moles and sunburned noses can benefit from a coat of concealer before applying foundation.

When choosing a foundation, pick a color that is as close to your normal skin tone as possible. Make sure to change the color to a darker shade in the summer if you tan. If you have oily skin, choose a drier foundation. Using a sponge to apply the foundation will give you a smooth and even texture. Make sure to apply the foundation down your neck and even to your chest if you have a lot of freckles. There is nothing worse than a "mask" look. Blending is key when it comes to makeup, so be sure to blend the lines where the concealer and foundation meet.

Step three: powder. You can use two different types of powder: loose and pressed. Pressed powder comes in a compact and is a lot handier than loose powder in the field. Which to use is really a matter of personal preference. Whichever you choose, a large cosmetic pad is the best way to apply it.

Be sure to shake off the excess powder on the pad first, then pat the powder on all over your face, neck and, if necessary, chest. Do not rub the powder on.

A heavier powder close to the color of your foundation is recommended for initial application. Translucent powder is excellent for touch-ups because it is lighter and will not "cake" as heavily after several applications.

Step four: blush and shading. Choose a blush that complements your skin tone. The fairer the tone, the lighter the blush. Light pinks and peaches are good for light-skinned blondes or redheads. Women with medium skin tones can use colors with more bronze in them. African-American women should use blush with rosier shades deeper in color.

When applying blush, use a bigger brush than the one that normally comes in a compact. This will give a softer, more even application. Blush can be used for other areas besides the cheeks. A light dusting around the jaw line, the temple and forehead area, and even under the eyebrows can give the face a nice glow. Just be careful not to apply too much anywhere. Again, blending is the key.

Shading is an excellent product for slightly changing the shape of your face by adding contour. It looks like a light brown blush. There are brushes specifically for shading that are helpful for the cheek area. To accentuate cheeks and make the face look thinner, apply shading under the cheekbones, blending it with the blush.

Shading is also useful to give your nose a sharper look. Using a small brush, like the type used for eye shadow, put a light amount of shading on both sides of the bridge of your nose. Make sure to blend the edges so you don't see the actual lines on your nose.

Eyes:

Step one: eye shadow. Eye shadow should accentuate your eyes, not overpower them. Any color that blatantly stands out is distracting for television. Unless you're covering a special event like the Oscars, keep it simple.

The old adage that your eye shadow should match your eye color went out a long time ago. Just because a person has blue eyes doesn't mean she should wear blue eye shadow. In fact, no one should wear blue eye shadow on television. Earth tones are good for just about any eye color. Grays and charcoals can be nice, as well as plums and lilacs. You can vary your colors to match what you are wearing; however, you can never go wrong with simple earth tones.

Use a light creamy color for the entire lid. To give lift to the eyes, use a darker color in the crease and at the outer edge of the eye socket. Applying a lighter color under the eyebrow helps to open the eye area and makes your eyes stand out better. This technique is especially useful for women with narrowly shaped eyes. As I mentioned before, a little blush under the outer portion of the brow can add a nice glow.

When you're finished, make sure to dust away any shadow that may have fallen under your eyes during the application. If necessary, touch up with a little powder.

Step two: liner. As with eye shadow, liner should be used to accentuate the eyes and should not stand out on its own. Generally it is applied to the top lid above the lashes and very lightly under the lower lashes. Using too much liner will darken your eyes and create a much harsher look, which is not what you want for television.

There are three types of liner: liquid, pencil or pressed powder. Eye shadow can be used in place of pressed powder liner and is applied the same way, using a brush with a little water. Black eye liner is extremely harsh and should only be used on people with darker skin and eyes. Brown and charcoal liners tend to be nicer because of their softer tones. No matter what color you use, make sure to smudge the liner so you don't see harsh lines painted on.

If you have so-called "puppy dog" eyes (a shape that droops a little at the end), don't bring the liner all the way to the end of the lid. Instead, stop three-quarters of the way, bringing the line up slightly. Then blend that with the darker shade of eye shadow on the edge of the eye. Keep everything under where your eyebrow ends. This will add lift to the eye and take away the droopiness.

Under the eye, keep it light. Another trick to avoid a "heavy" look is to only carry the liner three quarters of the way from the outside in.

Step three: mascara. Black or dark brown are generally the best colors for television. If you're going to be out in the field and your eyes have a tendency to tear up in the cold or wind, use waterproof mascara. Using an eyelash curler before applying mascara helps to make the eyes stand out more. Another trick to lift the eyes is to apply more mascara on the upper outer lashes, or even better, to apply single false eyelashes in that area. This is tricky, so practice doing this when you're not pressed for time.

Step four: eyebrow shading. Use a small brush and apply an eye shadow that is close to your brow color. You can also use a pencil in the same manner. The idea is just to accentuate the brows, so apply the shadow very lightly. It's important to keep your brows neatly plucked or waxed, but don't go overboard. Eyebrows that have to be completely "painted" on are not attractive.

Lips:

Step one: liner. Lining your lips can give you a fuller look and help your lipstick last longer. The best way to keep lipstick from disappearing too quickly is to powder the lips first, then line them, using the liner to shade in the lip area, then powder lightly again, then apply lipstick. For women with thinner lips, apply the liner just on the outside of the lip to achieve a fuller look. Make sure the colors of the liner and lipstick are close in shade. You don't want the liner to stand out.

Step two: lipstick. Lipstick is best applied with a brush. Choosing a color can be difficult. You don't want something too bright, but if it's too neutral, it will look like you don't have lips under those bright lights. Generally, blondes look better in shades of pink and peach and look terrible in bright red and dark plums. Just because you're wearing a bright red jacket, doesn't mean you should wear bright red lipstick. Instead, look for a tone that has more pink in the red. Women with darker or red hair can handle darker shades of red or plum. Watch out for lip gloss. Heavy gloss will reflect the lights and make your lips look glassy. Again, just as with the rest of your makeup, you don't want your lips to stand out to the point of distraction. Instead, the color you choose should complement your skin tone and the colors of your clothing.

Makeup for Men

Base Makeup:
   Step one: moisturizer. It is just as important for men to use a moisturizer as it is for women. Even if you are only applying powder, using a lightweight lotion on your face will give the makeup a smoother look.
   Step two: concealer and foundation. These are products that many men will only need for in-studio work. However, for men who tend to have circles under their eyes, it is a good idea to use a little concealer in the field. Choose a concealer that is lighter than your foundation. Often just a couple of shades lighter will do. Apply it under the eyes with a makeup sponge or your index finger, and also use it to conceal any blemishes or scars on the face.
   When choosing a foundation, pick a color as close to your skin color as possible. If you tan, make sure to use a darker color that matches your skin tone at the time. If you have oily skin, ask for a foundation that has less oil in it. The best products to buy are those made specifically for television use. Beauty supply or MAC makeup stores are generally better than department stores for these items.
   Applying makeup for the first time is always tricky for men, simply because it's all new to them. The best advice for men is to seek advice the help of female colleagues; they will be happy to help.
   Application of both products is the same for men and women. Use a makeup sponge to apply foundation, spreading

it evenly over the face and neck. Make sure to blend the edges of the concealer into the foundation. Be sure to tuck tissues around your shirt collar to prevent any of the makeup from getting on the edge. You will most likely have makeup residue on the inside of your shirt collars, so make sure to point it out to the cleaners so they can spot the area before laundering the shirt.

Step three: powder. Whether in the field or studio, men should always have powder on hand. It's the best way to get rid of shiny areas on the face, like those on the nose and forehead. For men, a compact generally works best and is easiest to use. Pressed powders that are a mix of foundation and powder provide excellent coverage with just one product. Use a cosmetic puff to apply the powder. The larger puffs tend to work better than the smaller ones that come with the powder. Apply powder by rubbing it onto the puff, shaking off the excess, then patting it around the face. Make sure to blend it in so you don't see any powder residue on the face.

As for using blush and shading on men, there are several schools of thought. I think it's generally a bad idea because it's very difficult for it to look natural on men. If you want to add color to your face, a better trick is to apply bronzer to your face before putting on the foundation and powder. This will give you a natural glow and will diminish the risk of you looking like a clown.

Eyes and Lips:

I've seen makeup artists use mascara and lip gloss on men, and the result is never good. It always shows, and looks plain girly! Don't use anything other than concealer, foundation and powder around your eyes.

As for the lips, use a lip balm to give them a moisturized look. This helps make them more visible to the camera. Lipstick and gloss are just not necessary.

Bottom Line: Keep It Simple

The key to a good look for television is simplicity. Anything that distracts the viewer is bad. Bold makeup, chunky jewelry and big hair are out. The good news for women is that they are no longer expected to have the proverbial "anchor do." Simple and neat styles that are easy to manage are best. The same applies to jewelry as well. Smaller earrings and necklaces are much nicer than bigger and busier jewelry.

Finally, don't keep changing your style. Once you find a look that you're comfortable with on camera, keep it. This will make your life easier as well. When news is breaking, you don't have a lot of time to spend on your makeup and hair. Having a consistent look that you have down pat will help you spend more time working on your newscast than on your makeup.

The Bad Hair Day

How many times have you seen a reporter whose hair is standing straight up on a windy day? An anchor with a strand of hair out of place or falling into his or her eyes? This is very distracting; the television viewer tends to pay more attention to the hair problem than the story. The general rule: make sure your hair is clean, neat and away from your face. It's been said that the hole in the ozone layer has been single-handedly caused by television news people's use of hairspray. In our business it's a necessary evil.

In television, before you radically change your look, keep in mind that the station has most likely invested in promotional photos and on-air imagery. You may even be featured on billboards or print ads that can't be changed. The right thing to do is ask your manager if it's okay to make a hairstyle change.

CHAPTER 7

On-Air Delivery

The viewer watches me and chooses to believe that I believe what he believes.

Ted Koppel

It's Not What You Say, It's How You Say It

You get into an argument in the newsroom or at home. Your voice changes; you make faces or gestures. In private your only critics are those with whom you are arguing. On the air, however, your delivery can expose you to public ridicule or worse, because the expression on your face or in your voice is open to interpretation.

In writing for *Communication Lawyer*, Catherine Van Horn and Steven Mandell point out that television allows for the use of vocal inflections to add power to the message. The example they cite is from a special report on the sale of liquor to minors put together by WFLD-TV in Chicago. The station was sued by one of the subjects of the report. The report first depicted a sixteen-yea-old girl placing telephone orders with a number of local liquor stores. The report then showed the drivers delivering the alcoholic beverages to the minor without asking for identification, or even questioning her age. In the final segment the plaintiff of the suit is shown placing a keg of beer inside the vestibule at the minor's address, accepting cash from the minor and walking back to his car. At this point the reporter and his cameraman confronted the plaintiff. The reporter then summarized the plaintiff's explanation of his actions. The plaintiff insisted to the reporter that he had carded the girl and was just leaving to move his car, which was doubled parked, so he could come back and wait until an adult showed up.

In this case no question was raised as to whether the reporter accurately reported the plaintiff's explanation. The plaintiff could be heard giving his explanation under the reporter's voiceover track. However, the plaintiff claimed that the reporter used an "incredulous" and "skeptical" tone of voice to report the plaintiff's explanation, and thereby gave a falsely negative impression of what had occurred.

The plaintiff's defamation action against the television station was based solely on the reporter's tone of voice. At first the U.S. District Court denied the television station's motion to dismiss, but later on reconsideration the court granted the motion. In doing so the court said a defamation action could not be based on voice inflection alone.

The authors of the article cite three other cases in which reporters were sued over the tone of their voice. Even though the plaintiffs didn't prevail in these cases, they took months or years to resolve and became very expensive. The television stations and reporters spent countless hours defending their actions and the legal fees were sizeable.

Controlling Voice Inflection

Dr. Ann Utterback is one of the world's leading voice coaches. She coaches many of our industry's most talented journalists on how the inflection in their voice can change the intended meaning of a story.

As a broadcast voice specialist, every day I observe how delivery can affect the reporting of a story. Consider this example: one of my clients was covering a case that involved a known drug dealer in Washington, D.C. This man was notorious for his blatant drug-related killings and his use of young teens as drug runners. My client spent weeks sitting in court covering this case.

Much to her surprise, the drug dealer began having notes sent to her in the courtroom saying he found her attractive. Obviously, my client's feelings of outrage were off the scale.

The challenge she faced was how to voice her packages and do her live shots without her feelings affecting her read. She knew she had to keep her emotions out of her reporting. During the trial, she could not let any emotion come through in her voicing. Even when he was found guilty, she had to keep her objectivity as a reporter. This example illustrates that broadcast delivery may be challenging in many ways.

When an anchor or reporter loses his or her voice, it is obvious that there is a vocal problem. Likewise, if viewers have complained about the quality of an on-air person's voice, it is a problem. But vocal problems are not just physiological, and they may not be immediately obvious. How an anchor or reporter uses voice to convey meaning may create a problem as well. This can happen when on-air broadcasters do not consider the emotions of what they are saying, how their voices may be revealing an inappropriate emotion or leaving an important emotion out.

For years, communication theorists have studied how meaning is conveyed through delivery. One well-respected study, done in the 1960s by social scientist Albert Mehrabian, concluded that as much as 93 percent of meaning in communication is nonverbal. His research showed that only seven percent of meaning comes through the actual content of the words. And of the 93 percent that is nonverbal, 38 percent of meaning comes from an area called *paralanguage*, all the vocal qualities of how we say words. (The additional 55 percent involves body language, specifically facial expressions, which also affects broadcast delivery.) Paralanguage includes vocal inflections, rate, articulation, volume, etc. In other words, how something is said and not what is said often makes the stronger impression.

How we say things is linked to emotion. Several years ago, I gave a lecture to several hundred news directors on sounding more conversational on the air. Part of this lecture involved talking about emotion in delivery. I truly thought that when I came to this part of my lecture, all five hundred news directors would leave the hall en masse. This is because for many years you could not put the word "emotion" in the same sentence with the word "news." In his book *Now the News*, Ed Bliss describes how in 1969, Spiro Agnew spoke out against "'a gaggle of commentators' swaying public opinion" with their voices. This created a fear that anything but a straightforward, serious delivery would always be inappropriate. But there is a difference between being "impartial" and being "insensitive."

The most important point when talking about voicing emotion in the news is that one should only voice *universal emotions*. When I explained this concept at my lecture, all the news directors agreed with me. Universal emotions are those reactions that we'd expect all our viewers to share. For example, everyone is sad when there is a natural disaster and thousands die. When children are killed, everyone's heart breaks. And if someone wins the lottery most of us are happy (envious, perhaps, but happy).

When problems arise is when the story is not about a universal emotion. Let's say a reporter is covering a court case involving a rape. The disgust the reporter may feel can creep into the delivery. This is not appropriate because all court cases are controversial by their very nature. So no matter how the reporter feels, he or she must remain objective.

The same thing was true for my client who covered the drug dealer. She was able to keep her reporting objective, but how could she have used her voice inappropriately? One of the most tempting ways would be to use a circumflex inflection. I call this the *Sixty Minutes* delivery. A circumflex means that you go up-down-up or down-up-down in pitch as you say a single word. Take the word "allegedly." If you say that word with a variation in pitch as you say it, you can contradict the meaning of the word. You can say it in a way that implies that the alleged criminal is guilty. Try it and see. Say the word and let your pitch change as you say it.

A common investigative reporting technique is to say something like, "The mayor refused to allow our cameras in her office." If you use the circumflex inflection on the word "refused," you will be making a nonverbal comment about the mayor's choice. This will mean that you are editorializing with your voice. Try reading the sentence with no change of pitch on "refused" and then with a circumflex inflection. Can you hear the editorializing?

Having a good broadcast voice goes beyond the basics of vocal quality and sounding conversational. It must also include a consideration of emotion and how it is conveyed. Any reporter or anchor can be caught in the trap of "editorializing" with the voice.

The Name Game

In print, it's simple: spell someone's name correctly. In broadcast it's a matter of pronunciation. During the many years that I anchored the news, especially when I first arrived in a market, I made mistake after mistake. The phones would ring off the hook with people correcting me. Many times, I had no idea I was pronouncing the name incorrectly. In western Pennsylvania I had the proper name "Custer" in my copy. I pronounced it like I would in the West (Custer's Last Stand). The phones lit up. It's *Coo-ster*, one woman said. The point is, make every attempt to pronounce names correctly and if you're not sure, ask. And, after you have been corrected, don't make the same pronunciation mistake twice.

But what about titles? When out on a local story always ask what title your subject wants next to/under his or her name in the supers or the article. More complicated situations come up from time to time as well. Remember the election of 2000. During the month of indecision, and then following the Supreme Court decision, journalists struggled with titles for George W. Bush. He was both governor of Texas and the president-elect for a brief period of time. In an e-mail one day Peter Jennings addressed the question of how to address the president of the United States on the air. Is it Mr. Bush or President Bush?

We find several of you asking about the way we refer to President Bush. "You keep referring to 'Mr. Bush,' instead of President Bush," someone writes. "Is that politically correct?" Another query goes like this: "I'm curious—at what point do you stop calling Bush 'The new president?'" Earlier on, during that 35-day limbo that followed Election Day, there were those among you who felt we should have called George W. Bush "President-elect." We never agreed with that—there was still a legal process to play out—but in this case, all right, we'll dispense with "the new president." As for "Mr. Bush"—if you read or listen carefully you'll notice we never refer to "Mr. Bush," or "Mr. Clinton" before him, without a first reference to "President Bush," etc.

William Randolph Hearst had a motto he lived by:
"Get it first, but get it right."

The Glancing Blow

If looks could kill. Facial expression, even if it's unintentional, is also a way to provoke negative reaction.

The raised eyebrow, the rolling eyes, the misplaced smile; all are open to public interpretation. It happens to just about every television anchor and reporter. Here's an example, which happened one night during the extended election of 2000. You may recall that Al Gore and George W. Bush were making nationally televised statements routinely during the Florida vote count and court activities. Just before the U.S. Supreme Court was to hear arguments, George W. Bush addressed the nation. Many thought that Peter Jennings made a face following the statement. Here's what he wrote in his daily e-mail on November 27, 2000:

We have had another example of what I think is "the eye of the beholder syndrome." There were a lot of e-mail messages today that suggested the look on my face after Bush spoke last night was disapproving—even biased. Actually, I was struck with the fact that it was a very serious moment and we treated it accordingly. But these messages remind me that as viewers we all bring our own biases to bear when we're watching news. Some years ago a professor concluded, in what he alleged was a serious survey, that every time President Reagan was on television, I smiled, therefore I was politically disposed to the president. I wondered at the time whether his college thought that was a worthwhile way to spend research money.

When a gesture or facial expression by a reporter or anchor is genuine and unrehearsed it can actually add to a listener's or viewer's experience. When you see the look of fear on a reporter's face, the audience can sense it. When an anchor reacts to a story with unmistakable joy, it can also be felt. I will never forget watching Walter Cronkite when the United States landed on the moon. Cronkite lowered his glasses and was so caught up in the moment he didn't know what to say.

Speaking to Kira Albin of *Grand Times*, Cronkite remembers:

I've said that I had as much time to prepare for that moon landing as NASA did, and I still was speechless when it happened. It just was so awe-inspiring to actually be able to see the thing through the television—that was a miracle in itself. And the successful landing...all I could say was, "Oh, boy...Whoo."

You Never Know When You're on the Air

So many buttons... All it takes is someone punching the wrong one in the control room and you're on the air when you're not supposed to be. The most embarrassing moments in broadcasting can come when

Courtesy KDNL-TV

a reporter or anchor is caught off guard this way. Blooper tapes kept by newsrooms around the country show anchors making faces, fixing their hair, picking at their teeth or worse. Earpiece failure leads to reporters not knowing they are live and we've all seen what has happened.

A famous clip passed around the industry shows a reporter waiting to do a set piece on a Chicago news set. The technical director inadvertently took the wrong camera just as this reporter was giving the finger to someone in the studio. It was embarrassing to say the least. But, in one of the quickest retorts ever, the main anchor said, "As our reporter showed you, we're number one."

Here are a few simple rules that can help you avoid such an on-air disaster:

- Be prepared for anything.
- Watch your actions.
- Don't act like a fool or try to be funny when it's not part of the broadcast.
- Always act responsibly when a camera is pointed at you or you're in front of a microphone.

Brian Williams forgot one of these cardinal rules of broadcasting one night when he filled in for Tom Brokaw on *NBC Nightly News*—he assumed a microphone was off. During a break in the East Coast broadcast of *Nightly* following a report on the death of Western movie actress Dale Evans, viewers heard Mr. Williams make an off-the-cuff comment saying that Trigger jokes would inevitably follow. Although there were some red faces at the network, there was also great relief that Mr. Williams—who fancies himself a comedian—didn't himself make a joke about the iconic cowgirl riding into the sunset one last time and thus didn't need to make formal apologies.

CHAPTER 8

Taking Liberties

Our liberty depends on the freedom of the press, and that cannot be limited without being lost.

Thomas Jefferson

C ongress shall make no law respecting an establishment of religion, or prohibiting the free exercise thereof; or abridging the freedom of speech, or of the press; or the right of the people peaceably to assemble, and to petition the Government for a redress of grievances."

The First Amendment of the United States Constitution protects the right to freedom of religion and freedom of expression from government interference. Freedom of expression consists of the rights to freedom of speech, press, assembly and to petition the government for a redress of grievances, and the implied rights of association and belief. Here's the catch: *the Supreme Court has the right to interpret the extent of the protection afforded under these rights.*

The First Amendment has been widely interpreted by the Supreme Court over the years. A lawyer in constitutional law would explain that the court has interpreted the due process clause of the Fourteenth Amendment as protecting the rights in the First Amendment from interference by state governments. Thus, the Court gives itself even more latitude to make First Amendment decisions.

Despite popular misunderstanding, the right to freedom of the press guaranteed by the First Amendment is not very different from the right to freedom of speech. This allows individuals to express themselves through publication and dissemination. It is part of the constitutional protection of freedom of expression. It does *not*, however, afford members of the media any special rights or privileges not afforded to citizens in general.

Hidden Cameras

Hidden camera and microphone reports have been the subject of much controversy over the years. There are state and federal laws regarding invasion of privacy, wiretap and eavesdropping. These laws protect journalists, sometimes at a cost. Anyone can sue if they feel their rights were violated, and many times they do.

Cameras have become smaller and smaller over the years and hidden camera journalism has become a mainstay of investigative television journalism. Many critics say that hidden cameras are being used too aggressively. Many viewers are now concentrating on the practice of using hidden cameras rather than on the information being uncovered.

One of the most infamous examples of hidden camera investigative reporting is the Food Lion report that aired in 1992 on ABC's *Primetime Live*. The program was sued in a landmark case. The Food Lion lawsuit raised serious questions about the practice of many television news organizations that send reporters and producers undercover with hidden cameras.

Here's the story:

Two ABC producers, while working undercover at Food Lion, secretly videotaped other employees for a *Prime Time Live* story that exposed food-handling practices and accused the grocery chain of selling rat-gnawed cheese and rotting meat. The report alleged that Food Lion employees had ground out-of-date beef along with new beef, bleached rank meat to remove its odor and re-dated products not sold before their expiration date.

Food Lion sued the network and won the first round in a landmark court trial. The jury found that ABC News was guilty of using fraudulent tactics. Although Food Lion denied the story's accuracy, it did not go after ABC for libel or slander. Instead, it sued for fraud, trespass and breach of the duty of loyalty, saying undercover reporters lied to get jobs and then wore spy cameras and hidden recorders.

The issue before the court had nothing to do with the actual documentation of wrongdoing by the store; jurors *never* saw a tape of the report that aired on ABC. Instead, they were asked to decide whether or not the show producers committed fraud by falsifying job applications to gain access to the store in order to do their report. The jury concluded that they had and should be punished. The award stunned some because it appeared to open a new line of legal attack against the news media and hidden-camera journalism that did not center on the veracity of the story. The reason the lawyers chose this line of attack against the television network was because libel and slander cases are harder to win when the story reported is found to be true.

Later, when the case went to appeal, a federal appeals court threw out the $315,000 judgment against ABC.

The 4th U.S. Circuit Court of Appeals in Richmond, Virginia, by 2-1, reversed a jury verdict that said ABC had committed fraud. The federal court also reduced the $5.5 million in punitive damages. The only financial award the court allowed was a nominal $2—$1 against each of the ABC producers.

The court determined that no fraud claim existed because Food Lion was not injured by the ABC employees' deception. And the court disagreed with the jury's finding that ABC engaged in a business deception in violation of the North Carolina Unfair and Deceptive Trade Practices Act, or UTPA.

"The deception...did not harm the consuming public. Presumably, ABC intended to benefit the consuming public by letting it know about Food Lion's food handling practices," said the opinion by Judge M. Blane Michael.

"Moreover, ABC was not competing with Food Lion, and it did not have any actual or potential business relationship with the grocery chain," so the law could not be used in this case, Michael wrote. Judge Diana G. Motz joined his opinion.

In dissent, Judge Paul V. Niemeyer wrote that there was ample evidence to support the jury's finding of fraud.

Food Lion, which is based in Salisbury, North Carolina, said it was disappointed. "This is a complicated legal area, and our lawyers will review the court's decision and advise us of our options," it said in a statement.

ABC News president David Westin described the appeals court's action as "a victory for the American tradition of investigative journalism."

"All of us can be reassured that the First Amendment continues to protect investigative journalists from attempts to intimidate them through threats of outlandish damage claims," Westin said in a statement.

Perhaps the bigger winners here were the attorneys. The legal cost in this case was in the millions.

One year later, same network, same program, different case.

Another hidden camera report was used by ABC's *Prime Time Live* program for a 1993 expose on whether employees at a psychic hotline believed in the service. An ABC reporter had gotten a job at the Psychic Marketing Group, which advertised telephone psychic advice for $3.95 a minute.

The employees of the company sued ABC under a federal eavesdropping law that allows people to tape conversations in which they are a party, unless the taping is intended to help commit a crime or damage another person.

The former employees also accused ABC of fraud, defamation and invasion of privacy under California law. Those claims were dismissed because they were added after the deadline to sue.

A federal judge ruled for ABC on the eavesdropping claim, concluding that recording a conversation for newsgathering purposes would not violate the wiretapping law.

The 9th U.S. Circuit Court of Appeals upheld the ruling. "Journalists do not get a blanket exemption," the appeals court said, "but taping for news-gathering purposes does not violate the law so long as there was no accompanying unlawful goal."

The case was appealed. The former employees said ABC committed a number of offenses under California law, such as fraud and invasion of privacy. The network therefore could be held liable under the eavesdropping law, the appeal said. ABC's lawyers said state law provided no remedy for the type of damage claimed by the employees.

The Supreme Court refused to revive the lawsuit by the 16 former employees. The court, without comment, turned away the former employees' argument that they should be allowed to sue ABC under a federal eavesdropping law.

However, a word of caution: there have been cases where television stations and networks have been compelled to settle lawsuits or pay awarded damages. Both ABC stories were good journalism, but at a cost. The legal fees alone were in the hundreds of thousands of dollars. Insurance paid the bulk of the fees in both cases. The network insurance premiums climbed and the insurance carrier wanted safeguards to protect their exposure in the future.

The use of hidden cameras will be debated for all time. Some say journalists should never lie, even to get the "Big Story." The ethics behind all this lie deep within the role that the journalist plays in today's society. The decision to use questionable means to break a story goes to the very heart of a reporter's personal values. If you choose to use these means, you must prove that there was no intent to harm innocent people. Whenever an innocent person is harmed, it damages journalistic integrity.

Before you invade a citizen's privacy or attack a business, carefully look at Chapter 9: Exposure.

Using Unnamed Sources

The words "sources say" is an open invitation to question a reporter's good work. Using a single unnamed source is always risky. It's best to hear from two or more sources before running a story. But in many cases one source is all you have. When this happens you must feel 100 percent confident in your own mind that the source is accurate and reliable. The best test of this is if you have successfully used that source before or you have taken your information to a manager and he or she has agreed that the source is sound enough for the story to run. You can't attribute information to an unnamed source, so if anything goes wrong you're on your own.

The four rules recommended by the Poynter Institute are:

- A story that uses confidential sources should be of overwhelming public concern.
- Before using an unnamed source, you must be convinced there is no other way to get the essential information *on the record*.
- The unnamed source must have verifiable and first-hand knowledge of the story. Even if the source cannot be named, the information must be proven true. If you are unsure the information is true, admit your uncertainty to the public.
- You should be willing to reveal to the public why the source cannot be named and what promises if any the news organization made in order to get the information

Many stories are written and reported that quote general, unnamed sources. The same rules apply. An example of this is how *USA Today* and the *Denver Post* reported on the Columbine shooting. Here is the article from *USA Today*—note passages highlighted in **boldface**:

LITTLETON, Colo.—The alleged gunmen in the school shooting here were unnamed for most of the day, but students at Columbine High School seemed to know them well.

They were described in angry terms as loners, outcasts and "satanic individuals" that billed themselves as the "Trench Coat Mafia."

The Denver Post, **quoting law enforcement sources and neighbors**, reported the names of the two dead suspects as Dylan Klebold, 17, and Eric Harris, 18, both Columbine students. No suicide note or declaration of motive is known to have been found.

"Columbine Aftermath"—Courtesy the Associated Press

Neighbors described the two as quiet kids from nice families who never caused much trouble. And **school authorities said** the students had not been disciplinary problems.

If the "law enforcement sources" had been wrong, you can imagine the liability the *Denver Post* would have faced.

While the newspapers had to wait until their next editions were published to release the information, television was *live*. Angie Kucharski, news director of KCNC-TV, recalls how her station became the first to report the identities of the two shooters:

As students ran from the school, they identified two other students who they said had been doing the shooting. We refrained from naming these students on-air until we were able to confirm by multiple sources that these two were the suspects and that they had died.

In a breaking news situation like Columbine, information is coming into the newsroom at an astounding rate. It's important that journalists remain calm and collect the information in an orderly manner. Many newsrooms have a disaster plan that includes specific assignments ("battle stations," if you will) so the information is confirmed and put on the air quickly and precisely.

Paying The Price for Your Silence

Exercising the rights afforded by the First Amendment, reporters often will not reveal their sources. This is when the Fifth Amendment kicks in and things can get messy. In some situations, a journalist's liberty can actually be taken away.

Some judges have little or no tolerance for reporters who won't reveal a source. Reporters who appear before them often end up in jail. Here are some examples of reporters who paid the price, as compiled by the Reporter's Committee for Freedom of the Press:

- **Sarah Owens**, Charlotte, N.C., WCNC-TV reporter. Found in criminal contempt in 1998, sentenced to 30 days in jail for refusing to testify about statements made by a murder suspect's attorney. After the attorney's testimony yielded the information prosecutors sought, the judge reduced her sentence to time served, which at that point was approximately two hours.

- **Bruce Anderson**, editor of *Anderson Valley Independent*, Calif. Found in civil contempt in 1996; jailed for total of 13 days for refusing to turn over original letter to the editor received from prisoner. After a week, he tried to turn over the letter, but judge refused to believe it was the original because it was typed. After another week, judge finally accepted that the typewritten letter was the original.
- **Felix Sanchez** and **James Campbell**, Houston, Texas, newspaper reporters, locked in judge's chambers for several hours in 1991; had refused to stand in the back of courtroom and identify possible eyewitnesses to crime. Appeal successful through habeas corpus petition.
- **Tim Roche**, Stuart, Fla., newspaper reporter. Subpoenaed in 1990 to reveal source for leaked court order supposed to have been sealed. Jailed briefly, released pending appeal. Later sentenced to 30 days for criminal contempt. Served 18 days in 1993 and was then released.
- **Libby Averyt**, Corpus Christi, Texas, newspaper reporter. Subpoenaed in 1990 for information about jailhouse interview. Jailed over a weekend; released when judge became convinced she would never reveal her source.
- **Brian Karem**, San Antonio, Texas, TV reporter. Subpoenaed by defense and prosecution in 1990; refused to reveal name of individuals who arranged jailhouse interview. Jailed for 13 days. Released when sources came forward.
- **Roxana Kopetman**, Los Angeles, newspaper reporter. Jailed for six hours in 1987 for resisting prosecution subpoena seeking eyewitness testimony. Appealed; court ruled against her, but criminal case was long over.
- **Brad Stone**, Detroit, Mich., TV reporter. In 1986, refused to reveal identities of gang members interviewed several weeks prior to cop killing. Jailed for one day; released pending appeal. Grand jury then dismissed.

- **Chris Van Ness**, California, free-lancer writer. Subpoenaed in 1985 in connection with John Belushi murder. Jailed for several hours; revealed source; released.
- **Richard Hargraves**, Belleville, Ill., newspaper reporter. Jailed in 1984 over a weekend in connection with libel case. Released when source came forward.

When doing a story with the potential to end up in criminal or civil court, look forward and do an analysis of what your personal exposure could be. The First Amendment and shield laws can only protect you so far and the rest is up to you.

A reporter's word is his or her bond. If you guarantee that you will keep a source's identity confidential, be prepared to do so and to accept the consequences. You can always ask a source if you would be permitted to reveal his or her identity if you were forced by a court order or other legal action. If the answer is no, then you must be willing to honor your source's request. The same applies to documents that you have received confidentially.

Gag Orders

We often hear about judges issuing gag orders in an attempt to keep the media at arm's length from an important story. Gag orders usually prevent lawyers and other people involved in a court case from commenting to the media. Here's an example in which I was involved. You may remember the case of the "Internet Twins," the bizarre story of a Saint Louis mother, Tranda Wecker, who put her twin girls up for adoption through an Internet company—twice. First to a California couple, and then to a couple in England.

The California couple, Richard and Vickie Allen, challenged the adoption of the twins by Alan and Judith Kilshaw of Wales. The Allens said that they had paid a California Internet broker $6,000 for the twins but that Tranda Wecker had taken the babies from them to resell them to the Kilshaws. The Kilshaws say they paid the same Internet broker $12,000 to adopt the girls in Little Rock, Arkansas.

Next, an Arkansas court ruled that the Kilshaws' adoption was invalid because Tranda Wecker had failed to meet the state's 30-day residency requirement. The Allens dropped their claim after Richard Allen was charged with molesting two of his children's babysitters.

Courtesy KDNL-TV

He has pleaded not guilty. The story became a media feeding frenzy as journalists in America and Britain competed to report each development.

A legal battle ensued and the case of the Internet twins landed in a British court. After hearing both sides and petitions from the Weckers' attorneys, the judge in England decided to send the babies back to biological parents in Saint Louis.

The twins arrived back in Saint Louis under a shroud of secrecy. On the following Saturday morning, I received a call at home: one of my reporters had received a tip that the twins were going to be reunited with their biological parents at a counseling center. I dispatched a crew to cover the event. No other media showed up; the parking lot was virtually empty. My reporter and photographer, fearing that they were in the wrong place, approached the building and were immediately met by undercover police who were not thrilled that they were there. My crew was told they could not come on the property but would have to shoot any video from the street. The babies and parents arrived and left and we had an exclusive. The judge in the case held a hearing that next Monday and issued a gag order. Here's how it was reported in the *Saint Louis Post-Dispatch*:

An angry St. Louis judge has slapped a gag order on the parents and attorneys of 9-month-old twins who were at the center of an international custody battle after a local television station videotaped the twins over the weekend.

St. Louis Circuit Judge Steven Ohmer has barred those connected with the case from discussing details with the media. Ohmer was angry that KDNL (Channel 30) aired footage of the girls being taken Saturday to a counseling center in midtown St. Louis, where their parents visited them.

At a closed hearing Monday, Ohmer made no changes to the living arrangements of the girls, who are currently in the custody of the Missouri Division of Family Services. The agency took protective custody of them Wednesday, 10 days after a British judge ruled that they be returned to the United States.

"We basically continued things as they are, with the children in protective custody," Ohmer said.

Ohmer, who has already sealed court files in the case, said he had placed a gag order on the case to avoid a media frenzy.

"I hesitated to do it, but it was the right thing to do," he said from his chambers. "I was disappointed with the visitation with the twins with both parents. We were trying to protect their privacy."

Ohmer said that he had planned on having some of the hearings open but that that was no longer his intention.

"We wanted it to work without it being a circus," he said. "We wanted the case to develop without a fishbowl atmosphere of the twins. They have to be given the opportunity to connect with their people so they can have a normal life. It can't be done in the glare of television cameras and reporters."

The twins' estranged parents, Tranda Wecker of St. Louis and Aaron Wecker of Arnold, arrived separately shortly after 1:30 p.m. to appear before Ohmer. About two hours afterward, Aaron Wecker emerged from the hearing with his live-in girlfriend and declined to comment.

"I can't say anything about the case because the judge has ordered us not to," he said.

His attorney, Bernhardt Klippel, said the Division of Family Services was conducting a study to determine where the girls would be placed permanently.

"Everybody is pleased with what has happened," Klippel said. "Today we just discussed the custody of the children."

Tranda Wecker's attorney, William Meehan, spoke to the media while his client stood silently behind him with her boyfriend, Michael Thompson.

"The parents are now trying to put together a parenting plan," Meehan said. "This is a progressive situation."

Other media including television and radio stations reported our actions and the issuance of the gag order. The question is, did we act in a responsible manner in the coverage of this story? Yes, because we abided by the rules the police set at the scene when shooting the arrival and departure of the twins. We shot the event from public property and made no attempt to follow the police motorcade once they had left this public facility. No harm came to any party involved in this story by the airing of this video. If other media outlets had been aware of reuniting of the parents with the twins, no doubt they would all have been at the scene as well. The judge in this case wanted future visitations to be private and ordered everyone involved in the case not to disclose locations in the future.

Challenging a Gag Order

If you feel a judge has gone too far in issuing a gag order and your company will back a legal challenge, here's how the First Amendment Handbook from the Freedom Forum recommends you handle it:

If a court issues a gag order in a case you are covering, the first thing you should do is obtain a copy. If it is a written order, the court clerk should be able to provide a copy. If not, you may have to pay to have the court stenographer transcribe the judge's oral directive.

Find out who the order gags and what restrictions it places on the gagged individuals. What is the judge's justification for issuing the gag? Nuances in the language of the order may greatly affect whether it will be upheld on appeal.

If the order prohibits you from publishing information you obtained during a court proceeding you attended, or information you obtained legally from a source outside the court, it is probably unconstitutional.

The Supreme Court of Kansas so ruled when it reversed the criminal contempt conviction of former *Atchison Daily Globe* publisher Gary Dickson in 1994. Dickson had violated a gag order by running front-page stories about the fact that the paper was ordered not to report on a drug defendant's criminal history, after a *Globe* reporter had attended an open preliminary hearing in the case.

The state Supreme Court ruled that the order was transparently unconstitutional. It warned, however, that the news media can be held in contempt for violating even an unconstitutional gag order if they fail to make a good faith effort to appeal before publishing. The court noted that Dickson and the *Globe* had met that requirement by trying—albeit unsuccessfully—to reach their attorneys and the issuing judge in the two hours prior to deadline.

However, federal appellate courts have disagreed on whether violating even unconstitutional gag orders is permissible.

In [a case involving the publication *Business Week*], the magazine and its publisher, McGraw-Hill, chose not to defy the federal court's gag order while it appealed the order. The trial court had ordered the magazine not to publish an account of documents it had received through an attorney.

The magazine appealed to the U.S. Court of Appeals (6th Cir.) as well as to U.S. Supreme Court Justice John Paul Stevens, in his capacity as Circuit Justice. Stevens refused to stay the injunction, finding that the magazine was first obligated to contest the order before the trial judge. He also ruled that the manner in which *Business Week* obtained the documents— whether it knew the documents were filed under court seal— might have a bearing on whether it had a right to publish them.

Regardless of your inclination when faced with a gag order, time is of the essence, and you should call your editor immediately to obtain legal counsel.

If your sources have been gagged, you will need advice on whether you can challenge the order or whether the person directly affected by it must bring the challenge. Here, too, you will need the help of legal counsel.

In some cases, a judge will lift or modify a gag order when told of the constitutional problems it poses. But a formal appeal may be necessary to protect your ability to cover a court case.

CHAPTER 9

Exposure

A true journalist...is fact-proof.

George Bernard Shaw

Every time journalists go on the air, put their words in print or even make personal appearances they are exposing themselves to potential liabilities. Just where do we draw the line?

Journalists live in a climate of lawsuits and legal challenges. Thousands (yes, *thousands*) of legal actions are taken against the media and individuals every year.

So you want to do an investigative report. You ask, what are the rules? What's my liability? Am I putting my employer in jeopardy?

This 2000 case clearly illustrates how careful journalists need to be. The case involved a Utah Television station using a hidden camera for an investigative report. Jim Rayburn of the *Deseret News* writes:

A jury's $3 million defamation verdict against KTVX Channel 4 will probably make Utah journalists more cautious and have a chilling effect on investigative journalism, a Utah media attorney says.

The award may be Utah's largest defamation verdict.

"This is by far and away the largest verdict I'm aware of," said Salt Lake media attorney Randy Dryer. "And this will certainly get everyone's attention, there's no doubt about that."

On Friday, a 4th District jury awarded $2.2 million in economic losses to Orem physician Michael H. Jensen for three stories KTVX ran in 1995 and 1996 on Jensen's practices of prescribing diet pills. The stories said Jensen violated Utah law and medical regulations when he prescribed fen-phen to former reporter Mary Sawyers without weighing her or giving her a physical, and when he suggested "maybe" prescribing Dexedrine, a non-diet medication, if the fen-phen did not work.

The jury found that Sawyers' stories defamed the doctor, cast him in false light and that his privacy was invaded by the use of a hidden camera.

"This verdict will have a chilling effect on editors and news directors, who will impose more caution and self-restraint on their reporters," Dryer said.

Monday the jury added about $840,000 in punitive damages, an amount less than most legal observers expected. Normally, punitive awards are much higher than compensatory awards. Also, California-based United Television, owners of KTVX and six other television stations across the country, has more than $500 million in assets.

The station decided to do a story on Jensen after an assistant news director said he witnessed Jensen prescribing fen-phen to the host of a Fourth of July party. News officials decided to have Sawyers pose as a patient and use a hidden camera after Jensen declined to prescribe diet medication to her over the telephone.

Sawyers took the hidden camera video to state licensing officials, who then filed a disciplinary petition against Jensen. Jensen was publicly reprimanded after agreeing to a stipulation that he had violated medical procedures for prescribing medication.

Before the petition was filed, however, and shortly after the first story aired, Jensen was fired from his job as a family practitioner and was denied insurance privileges from Intermountain Health Care.

Dale Gardiner, Jensen's attorney, told jurors that Jensen admits he had prescribed diet pills too freely. However, he said several segments of the stories and statements made by Sawyers were just simply false. Mainly, Sawyers said she caught Jensen on camera "promising me illegal drugs" when Jensen actually said "maybe" he'd be willing to prescribe Dexedrine. Jensen had also recanted that possibility and later told Sawyers he could not prescribe Dexedrine to her prior to the airing of the first story.

Dryer said from a legal standpoint the use of hidden cameras is much riskier than it used to be.

"This jury did what a whole series of juries are doing across the country in not looking favorably at the use of hidden cameras and other surreptitious means of gathering news," he said.

The verdict will also likely reinforce a trend of the media engaging in less investigative journalism.

"I think that is not a good development for the public, because the information gained from that kind of reporting is usually information the public should know," Dryer said.

Though admitting he violated regulations in prescribing fen-phen to Sawyers, Jensen said the news station clearly set him up. The hidden camera incident was the only complaint ever filed against Jensen, who now works as a physician at nursing homes in Salt Lake City.

"I took public issue with this, and I wasn't going to let this go without a fight," Jensen said.

He said his actions were motivated by his sincere care for a patient who turned out not to be a genuine patient. Jensen said he was led to believe that Sawyers was going to lose her job if she didn't lose weight.

Attorney Robert M. Anderson told jurors that the station stands by the stories and that the stories were basically true. He said Jensen suffered the consequences of his own conduct and not that of the station or Sawyers. Station officials say they have not decided whether to appeal the verdict.

This, of course, is just one case, and there are cases against journalists that are decided in their favor, but even these cases are not resolved without great legal expense.

The Pre-broadcast Review Process

Investigative journalism is the lifeblood of our industry, but the best investigative journalists are also the most careful.

When you go after the tough stories that involve risk, you have to weigh the potential exposure against the value of the end result of the report.

There are many guidelines to measure potential liability. On the following pages are some questions you must ask yourself when embarking on a potentially libelous story.

Richard Goehler, of the law firm Frost & Jacobs in Cincinnati, is one of the nation's leading media attorneys. When speaking to a small group of news directors at the Radio-Television News Directors Association meeting in Minneapolis, he shared his views on testing your story for liability. He came up with the "Pre-broadcast Review" which is the heart of this chapter. The review is in two parts. The first deals with actual broadcast, and the second deals with the writing and producing aspects of the story. Most of these principles also apply to the print media.

The liability guidelines in Goehler's Pre-broadcast Review should be an essential part of your personal journalistic ethic. Keep these tips handy and share them with your newsroom. The issues listed below can become matters of survival in the litigious age in which we live.

Identifying Potential Pitfalls and Avoiding Liability

1. Methods of pre-broadcast review depend largely upon journalistic objectives. If done properly, the pre-broadcast review can add precision of language, reduce risk of suit and demonstrate that extraordinary care has been taken.
2. Is it defamatory? Does the statement injure reputation? If so, can it be proved to be true?
3. Who are the potential plaintiffs (public or private)? Evaluate each separately.
4. Evaluate the sources. Is there only a single source? Is there a confidential source? Will he/she agree to go

public in case of a claim? Is there an untested source with no prior track record? Are there any inconsistencies among sources? How many solid, consistent sources are there?

5. Is there an applicable privilege (statutory or common law)?
6. Are there any privacy problems (false light, private facts, misappropriation)?
7. Are there any newsgathering problems (trespass, intrusion, misrepresentation, contact with source, etc.)?
8. Has the reporter remained objective?

Pre-broadcast Writing and Producing

A. Reports which are most prone to libel lawsuits
   1. False reports about criminal justice: reports of arrest, convictions and prior criminal records, particularly reports about drug abuse or drunkenness.
   2. False statements about certain "high risk" kinds of people: children, doctors, lawyers and other business and professional people who trade on their reputation; middle level public employees, teachers and school officials.
   3. False reports about private disputes between people
   4. False headlines, promos, teases or fonts that hype a news story
B. Editing practices that may lead to libel/privacy problems
   1. Oversimplification, compression, unfairness, headlines, promos or teases stronger than the story, and incorrect references to areas of technical expertise.
   2. Various "red flag" words and expressions typify the numerous words and expressions that may lead to a libel or privacy lawsuit if not carefully handled in a news story.
C. Special problems associated with advertisements—promos and teases
   1. Timing factor

2. Accuracy
3. Other possible "red flags":
   a. Use of file photos
   b. Improper juxtaposition of visuals and text
   c. Titles, question marks, etc.
D. Special attention to the issue of balance and fairness—
   problems created if this issue is ignored.
   1. Obvious bias
   2. Failure to interview critical witnesses
   3. Lack of meaningful opportunity to respond
   4. Failure to present both or all sides of the story

The Liability You Face Every Day

Attorneys look mostly for the intent by the reporter to harm a company or individual. Something you must always remember is this:

Anyone can sue for any reason.

Frivolous lawsuits happen every day, and whether there is a basis for the action or not, reporters still end up in court and cost their media outlets megabucks to defend. As a reporter you can end up in endless depositions and even end up sitting in the witness chair defending your actions. Many defendants in these suits see the media as having deep pockets. Many in our industry contend that if the public had a better understanding of how our business works, and all the cost-cutting that's going on, they would not file so many groundless actions.

We as journalists all do investigative pieces, many of them award winners. However, we don't carry around a book of rules and often don't consider the legal consequences of our actions. What we should do is keep the basics in mind and use common sense.

When writing your report, keep the endgame in mind. If you feel good about your story and believe that you're in the clear, go ahead. If there is the slightest bit of doubt as to any potential exposure, seek out a manager, editor or even an attorney before your story hits. I have heard throughout my career that if you ask an attorney, he or she will automatically try to kill the story. It's been my experience that any good lawyer will do just the opposite; he or she will try to make it happen for you.

CHAPTER 10

Getting Involved

The vision of a world community based on justice, not power, is the necessity in our age.

Henry Kissinger

You're A Public Figure, So Act Like One

The only difference between a politician who's out shaking hands to win supporters and a journalist who needs ratings is that most journalists like to stay behind the scenes. In reality the best-known and most remembered journalists are those who have a flair for being in the public eye and who get involved in the community.

As journalists we must remember that we are a part of the communities in which we live. We contribute to the local economy, socialize and drive on the same streets as everyone else. We are citizens, but we're also journalists. It is our obligation to report on what we see that's obviously wrong; however, we must balance that with reports on the good deeds and good projects.

To be a responsible journalist you must also be a responsible citizen. Contribute to at least one cause about which you feel strongly. Become involved in a local reading program to help illiteracy, the local humane society or helping the homeless. Pick a cause and lend your support.

During my time in Memphis I witnessed a growing crime problem that greatly concerned me, and I felt I must do something to help. So, "The Mid-South Night Against Crime" was born.

I contacted each television station and after a series of meetings convinced them to all participate in a one-hour simulcast.

The Mid-South Night Against Crime was a unique simulcast, and a project which had a profound positive impact on the city of Memphis. The program was well watched and well received, and set a record 30 rating/53 share (combined NSI overnight rating).

The hour-long simulcast took place on June 23, 1998 on WPTY-TV (ABC), WMC-TV (NBC), WREG-TV (CBS), WHBQ-TV (FOX), WKNO-TV (PBS), WLMT-TV (UPN) and several Time Warner cable channels.

Each station had assigned a producer who attended the planning meetings and implemented their station's stories. The final program was assembled by WPTY-TV and delivered to stations via satellite time provided by Federal Express.

Each of the stations produced segments on various aspects of crime in the Memphis area. The programs identified problems and offered solutions. 13 Reporters and 11 Anchors representing all the par-

Courtesy Night Against Crime

ticipating television stations took part in the project. Montel Williams provided the opening and closing statement. The program was followed by a two-hour town hall meeting on WKNO-TV (PBS) featuring community leaders and hosted by A&E's Bill Kurtis. Introductions to the reports were provided by news anchors from each of the stations.

The project was done in cooperation with the Memphis Police Department, The Shebly County Sheriff's Department, the Memphis/Shelby County Crime Commission and Crime Stoppers. The sheriff's department, Memphis police and the National Guard conducted the largest crime sweep in county history while the program was on the air. Police served over 300 fugitive warrants. The coverage of the arrests was carried live on each station's 10 p.m. news.

The program was made available at Memphis area Blockbuster Video stores and the public library. The program would also be distributed to public schools, community centers, churches and neighborhood watch leaders throughout Shelby County.

The response was overwhelmingly positive. The program won national awards and was a model for similar projects in other cities. We got involved; so can you.

If You Feel Strongly Enough...

If you feel strongly enough about a situation in your area, get involved, and make a difference. Hot-button issues like the environment or education can get a newspaper, radio or television station directly involved in the community. Getting involved can create a win-win scenario for both the media outlet and the public. Such was the case in Pensacola, Florida, as news director Peter Nuemann explains:

When Florida Governor Jeb Bush unveiled his school voucher and school grading program, it was immediately controversial. The voucher program was to be tested in the Pensacola area of Escambia County, Florida, 200 miles west of the capital of Tallahassee, and later employed in all 92 Florida counties. Parents of students in two failing ("F" Grade) schools were offered vouchers to send their kids to private schools at taxpayer expense.

Opponents of the vouchers, led by the local teachers union and the Democratic school superintendent, claimed the vouchers would drain needed resources and finances from the schools, ultimately meaning their demise. The teachers, of course, also opposed this because Governor Bush wants teacher accountability as a measure of what state monies go to which schools. Teachers have been pressing for better salaries, but it didn't appear that they would get them without testing, accountability, which they opposed.

When this unfolded, WEAR-TV's news team made an unusual commitment to the story, the schools and the community. We hosted an appreciation breakfast for the teachers at Spencer-Bibb, one of the two "F" Grade inner-city schools; we reported almost in minutia the effects of the vouchers on the school and individual families, the efforts to boost morale and performance; we helped grow community mentoring in after-school programs; we repeatedly talked to Governor Bush and his education commissioner about their goals for the vouchers. We knew that how well we told the story could impact hundreds of thousands of other students statewide. Almost every day for practically a year, our reporter Cindy Reeves told in detail the issues of the voucher program and all its ramifications.

Both "F" schools raised their grades significantly a year later and came off the failing schools list. The Florida courts held the voucher program to be unconstitutional. And the county's voters replaced the incumbent school superintendent with a conservative Republican high school teacher.

Now, in an effort to save money and provide teacher salaries, his school redistricting and reorganization plan includes the closing of both of the once-failing "F" schools, Spencer-Bibbs and A. A. Dixon.

Our coverage has helped give the viewer and the community the knowledge to make the best choices for our schools, and our community. Our coverage of education issues has been seamless, consistent, and thus fully in the context of responsible civic journalism.

Get Connected with Your Audience

When you're at the grocery store, ask people what news they watch and why. Ask what articles or parts of the newspaper they read regularly. Listen to what people are talking about while you're standing in line to check out. When you're at a restaurant or sporting event, listen to what's on people's minds. Don't be afraid to introduce yourself, tell people what you do for a living, and ask for their comments or advice. After all, we are in the business of communicating.

Become aware and read articles, like one written by Ed Fouhy, executive director of the Pew Center, which begins:

> I grew up in the golden age of newspapers. There were seven dailies published in the Boston of my youth. The city editor of one of them was my cousin Bob. As the civic journalism movement has developed, I have thought a lot about Bob and what cross currents have changed the world of journalism since he sat in the city editor's chair. Perhaps in those currents we might find the answer to why readers, viewers and listeners so rarely find their voices and their concerns reflected in the pages of the daily newspaper or on the six o'clock news.
>
> Part of the answer, I think, lies in the growing elitism of journalists and the distance we have put between ourselves and the people we serve.

The Pew Center comes out with yearly surveys that take the pulse of television viewers. The 2000 survey opens with this analysis:

> Local television news has reached a crossroad.
>
> Viewers are beginning to abandon the medium, especially to the Internet, much as network news began to lose audience more than a decade ago with the advent of cable.
>
> But in response the industry is headed toward making a fateful mistake.
>
> A major ongoing study of local television news reveals that the business is cutting back on precisely the elements that attract viewers—including enterprise, localism, breadth,

innovation, and sourcing. A major reason is that the business is committed to maintaining profit margins it enjoyed in an earlier era.

Without needing to, local television news is driving Americans away from what was long the most popular and trusted source of information in the country.

Time after time we are told that journalists have to reconnect with the public on which they report. But how do you do that? One unique idea came to me while watching *Gordon Elliot's Door Knock Dinners* on the Food Network: let's go right into the viewers' homes and ask them what's on their mind, and do it live. Thus "Bringing News Home" was born.

The first part of this project was to locate families to visit, with the object of using families from every ethnic group and from every income level. We also wanted to speak with families from every part of our viewing area. To achieve this we used area school systems and put together criteria for schools to help in selecting the families. After getting the leads from the schools, our producers interviewed the families, first by phone and then in person. We wanted to be sure they were not camera shy and had issues about which they felt passionate. Each family was briefed on how a live shot worked and what would be happening. We never prompted the family on what to discuss. This was to be a live forum. Certain family members even wore IFBs so they could ask questions to our anchors in the studio as they chose. This quickly became a learning experience for all of us, when the first night of the project didn't go as well as we would have liked. A member of the family was rambling; even their dog failed to show up on cue.

Here's how *Saint Louis Post Dispatch* TV columnist Gail Pennington reported on "Bringing News Home."

A TV anchor? In your living room? Is this a good idea?

Channel 30 news director Jeff Alan thinks it is, so weeknights during May sweeps he's dispatching anchor Patrick Emory into households throughout the metropolitan area under the banner "Bringing News Home." The result so far has been a lot of buzz—including some snickers—and a modest increase in viewership.

"Bringing News Home"—Courtesy the Associated Press

Sight unseen, the project suggests the cable series "Gordon Elliott's Doorknock Dinners." In that one, the Food Network host roams New York neighborhoods with a crew in tow, knocking on doors and asking to come in and cook dinner.

And in fact, Alan may have been subliminally influenced by "Doorknock Dinners," which he'd watched just a few nights before the idea for the project hit him in the middle of the night. Another trigger was a recent study showing that viewers are increasingly tuning out local TV news, in part blaming sensationalism.

"People tell us they want to see their own community on television more than they do," Alan says. "They tell us we only go where crime is and not where positive things are happening. We're supposed to be serving viewers, and maybe we aren't doing that."

For the Channel 30 project, billed as a "major news experiment," families were chosen via school systems throughout the metropolitan area, with a goal of having "every community and every type of family" represented.

Monday's heavily promoted debut segment in Chesterfield was something of a disaster, rambling and repetitive, with even the family dog failing to show up for its climactic moment in the spotlight. Alan acknowledges the problems, saying, "When we went in, we didn't really know what to expect. We're fine-tuning as we go along."

By Tuesday, when the Witherspoon family of St. Louis was featured, things went more smoothly, thanks in large part to the fact that Marvin and Robin Witherspoon had plenty to say.

Marvin Witherspoon, a captain in the St. Louis Fire Department, says his family was enthusiastic when asked to participate.

"People get wrong ideas about St. Louis, especially north St. Louis, from watching the news," he says. "It's human nature to thrive not on good things but on bad things, like crime, but it's unfortunate."

Robin Witherspoon, a teacher at Griffith School in the Ferguson-Florissant district, concurs, saying the family was glad for a chance to show a positive side of north St. Louis.

The down side: The couple's four children (Erica, 15; Brittanie, 14; Lauren, 12; and Marvin Jr., 9) didn't get a chance to speak, even though Marvin Jr.'s whole school had tuned in to see him. And the Witherspoon parents were taken aback by how they looked on television. "I'm not doing that again until I get out and do a lot more walking," Marvin Sr. said, complaining about pounds added by the camera.

All the Witherspoons are surprised at the response that followed the appearance. "We've been recognized in the grocery store and on the street and told that we had great comments," Robin said. "So people were not just watching but listening."

Alan, too, is surprised and pleased at reaction to the project.

"This thing has blossomed on me," he says. "The response has been overwhelmingly positive, the most positive response I ever remember on anything."

Although the station hasn't been keeping a log, Alan cites "at least 100 calls" praising the segments. The experiment has attracted attention from national trade publications like *Electronic Media* and from The Associated Press.

Wednesday night, about 11,000 more households watched Channel 30's 10 p.m. newscast than had tuned in the previous Wednesday. In addition, the station's audience share—the percentage of TV sets in use tuned to a particular program—was up 3 points.

Some of that increase might have been credited to the Witherspoons, if they were a Nielsen family. Usually Channel 5 viewers, "We've been watching ABC 30 this week," Robin Witherspoon said. "It's interesting to hear what other people are saying."

During the initial phase of the project we talked with single parents, grandparents raising children, a family who had lost their farm, a gay couple, children with disabilities and many other concerned citizens. All of this was very enlightening, thought-provoking and uplifting. We learned more about and from our viewers than we could have imagined. On several occasions our families asked questions of public officials. The next day we interviewed and received answers from these officials then aired them prior to going live to that night's family. The station continued the project with a new family each week, making their concerns public directly from their living room.

Public People, Private Lives

There is a downside to being such a visible part of your local community. Every time you go to dinner, attend an event or even walk down the street, someone may recognize you, so you must always remember to behave accordingly. As with any other public person, a journalist who becomes involved in questionable activities can *become* the news.

Here are some of the ugliest examples of how a journalist's bad judgment can turn into a public scandal:

- The *Atlanta Journal-Constitution* reported that an Atlanta television station has taken disciplinary action against a reporter following an off-color remark he made into an open microphone while the station was airing his news report. The station received at least 150 e-mails and more than 200 telephone calls about the outburst.

- As reported in *Electronic Media*, a longtime South Carolina news director is now no longer practicing journalism, but busing tables at a local restaurant as he awaits federal prosecution on embezzlement charges. He was arrested by the FBI and charged with misappropriating $11,500 in station funds to pay his American Express bill. However, an independent investigation by the station owner has allegedly turned up "financial irregularities exceeding $2.65 million dollars over a 12–13 year period."

- According to the *Times-Picayune*, a former New Orleans TV reporter has been arrested again on drug charges, this time in Florida. Police reports say that the reporter was arrested in West Palm Beach for possession of cocaine. This latest arrest should not affect his original plea arrangement of returning to jail on pedophile sex charges in New Orleans.

- Many national news sources reported that a Fox television news reporter, rushing to a live broadcast at the Florida Capitol, was arrested after driving his car into another journalist. A Florida Capitol Police officer arrested the reporter on "aggravated battery" with a motor vehicle, after he drove his car into a freelance journalist working in Tallahassee.

- From the *Nashville Tennessean*: It's just after midnight on Saturday, two days before Labor Day, and a busy part of town is still crowded with headlights. Near an intersection, blue lights are flashing and a police officer is standing on the roadside talking to a man he's just pulled over. The driver, a tall, heavy-set man, looks like a former football player now gone to seed. He seems a little unsteady and says he's had a couple of drinks, vodka or something. His license is at home. The officer notices that the man's right pant leg is soaked nearly to the knee, and the driver explains he had an accident in a portable toilet. Holding his arms out for balance, he tries to walk a straight line. He flunks but shows the officer that he's wearing a leg brace. The officer tells the suspect, who has refused a breath test, that he's under arrest for drunk driving. The man seems upset. Lit by the officer's spotlight, trousers wet, the driver at one point turns to the officer and says, "You know, I work for Channel 1 News." The suspect was Channel 1's news director!

All of the above stories happened in the span of a few months. From the extreme case of alleged embezzlement to a DUI arrest, careers were ruined. Years of valuable experience flushed down the drain, and for what? I won't preach; you know the rest!

The media make you into a god, then they kill you.
                                                    Richard Rutowski

CHAPTER 11

Hindsight

What should happen when you make a mistake is this: you take your knocks, you learn your lessons, and then you move on.

Ronald Reagan

If We Could Go Back and Do It All Over Again

One of the best ways to learn responsible journalism is to look back on the times we got it wrong. We can't change the past, but we can learn from our mistakes, and be more careful so they don't happen next time.

When a radio or television station is live, so much can go wrong, and often does. (For example, the Howard Stern fans who posed as officials and tricked countless news anchors including Dan Rather and Peter Jennings live on network television.) The competitive nature of the business gets the better of all of us from time to time. Case in point, a suicide on a Los Angeles Freeway carried live by most of the local television stations. If all the TV stations had agreed to have a delay system, this would not have happened. Competition and that "see it here first" attitude played a role in what became a hard lesson in responsible journalism.

The Associated Press reported:

Courtesy KTLA-TV

The camera didn't blink as Daniel V. Jones stopped on the freeway overpass, unfurled a banner, waved a gun, set fire to himself and then put a bullet in his head. Viewers, on the other hand, were horrified by the live images and furious at television stations that failed to cut away as Jones killed himself. "It's part of the unfortunate danger of live television," KCBS news director Larry Peret said. "When you have a guy with a shotgun in the back of his pickup and the freeway closed, that's a news story."

Cameras were trained on Jones, 40, for nearly an hour as he sat in the truck sipping from a can and petting a dog on the seat next to him. He got out of the truck at least twice to unfurl the banner, which read: "HMO's are in it for the money. Live free, love safe or die." Rush hour traffic was backed up for miles on several of the area's busiest freeways. The man leaped from his truck when it burst into flames, leaving the dog behind. He pulled off his burning clothes, went to the edge of the overpass as if to jump, then backed off, picked up a shotgun and shot himself. Some TV stations airing the scene live were unable to edit the graphic action, though

KCBS cut to a wide-angle shot as Jones appeared about to jump. "We did not anticipate this man's actions in time to cut away, and we deeply regret that any of our viewers saw this tragedy on our air," KNBC said in a statement. The KNBC feed was shown nationally by the MSNBC cable news channel. KTLA and KTTV had interrupted children's programming to cover the incident. KTLA asked viewers for "their understanding" for the upsetting and distressing images that can be broadcast in live news coverage. An unidentified receptionist at KCAL-TV quoted in the Los Angeles Times said the station received at least 120 calls during the incident, most asking the station to cut away. "We didn't like them seeing what they saw any more than they did," a KTTV spokeswoman said. KABC stuck with its afternoon broadcast of Oprah Winfrey's talk show, cutting away to the unfolding tragedy for brief updates. "We knew it was dicey because of the nature of the story," KABC news director Cheryl Fair said. She and her staff debated shifting to live coverage, but before they decided, Jones was dead. The station aired edited shots of the suicide scene immediately afterward. At a Burbank Airport terminal, there were shrieks and gasps of horror in a crowd that had gathered around a television set. Several mothers covered their children's eyes.

Jeff Wald, news director of KTLA, was standing in the feed area of the station as the events unfolded. His first impression when he saw the truck burst into flames with the dog inside was:

No one in his right mind would want to see his dog go up in flames, so it never occurred to me that this was an attempted suicide. He ran out of the burning truck and took his clothes off because they were on fire, so again, if he was trying to commit suicide, I don't know why he'd be running from the truck. The man then jumped onto the median and it looked like he might jump into oncoming traffic.

We then thought he was going to surrender because he was waving his arms madly and standing on the center divider, it looked to me like he wanted to give himself up. A few minutes later as he was walking around the freeway we noticed there was a shotgun in the back of the pick-up truck. He started going for it. At that point we had about seven seconds between the time he went for the gun and shot himself to get off of the picture. We screamed into the two-way radio to pull out; we tried to get off the picture, honest to God, and we just could not break away in time. We were so caught off guard because it just didn't make any logical sense to me that he was going to kill himself until that now famous seven seconds when we saw the gun. Obviously it would have been better not to show this at all.

According to Wald, all seven VHF stations and two Spanish language stations aired the live pictures of the suicide. KTLA and KTTV took much of the criticism for the event because they were in children's programming at the time.

Wald recalls the mood the day after:

All of us felt terrible that this picture got on the air. We're not really apologizing for the coverage because it's news and we have no control over a situation and we don't want to be in the censorship business. We don't need to bring pictures like this into kids programming, but we never thought it would develop into this. It gave us pause for a lot of soul searching. We had a meeting with the entire television station to talk about this event and to talk to each other about how to prevent something like this from happening in the future without shirking our responsibility to cover news as it happens and not allow competitive pressure to make those decisions for us.

Out of that meeting came a breaking news policy. According to Wald, the policy includes:

- The news director is the one to decide if the breaking news story warrants interrupting programming.
- The news director must alert the general manager, station manager or program director about the special report if it occurs during children's programming.
- If the interruption occurs during children's programming the station must air a special announcement that reminds viewers

that this is a special report and is no longer children's pro-gramming.

Wald said:

Even if you go though all the points in the breaking news policy, in this particular incident we probably would have reacted the same way. However, next time we will break away a lot earlier, leaving nothing to chance. In hindsight, the only thing I would have done differently is in that seven seconds if I was in the control room and not so far down the chain of command (in the feed area), I would have killed the picture in time. When something like this happens now, we are always prepared that the worst can happen. We remind our people to be ready to cut away.

Once you publish or air a news story, you're married to it and it's hard to get a divorce. There are stories that create media frenzies that you will look back on years from now and realize the impact they had. Remember West Palm Beach in the presidential election of 2000? If you pick up this book years from now you may not know what a Vote-A-Matic machine is. Voting by punch card may well be a thing of the past. Only the images of election officials holding punch cards to the light in search of "hanging chads" will remain in our minds and appear in the next generation of history books.

Setting a Bad Example

Not all examples of bad journalism start with questionable decisions or difficult situations. Many times it's a good idea that goes very wrong. Here's how CNN reported on an investigative report by a Columbus television station that shut down the Columbus airport for four hours, greatly inconveniencing thousands of travelers:

The FBI and the Federal Aviation Administration on Monday were investigating whether former federal trans-portation inspector general Mary Schiavo violated any laws in an airport incident in which hundreds of passengers were evacuated from a terminal and planes were pushed back from gates.

The evacuation occurred after Schiavo, a long-time critic of Federal Aviation Authority security measures, checked a bag on Friday at Port Columbus International Airport in cooperation with a story WCMH-TV was doing on airport security.

WCMH says Schiavo was working with the station to show how easy it is to slip a piece of unaccompanied luggage onto a domestic flight.

Schiavo said she bought a ticket to Washington, D.C., and checked her bag with America West Airlines, but did not board the flight. She said she was hoping to determine whether the bag would be allowed to take off with the flight even though its owner was not on board. The bag's discovery led to the shutdown of a runway for four hours.

Schiavo bought the ticket in her own name, she said, and had labeled the checked bag. It contained, among other things, a tape recorder, a sweat suit, a can of shaving cream and some children's modeling clay.

The station showed that the bag also contained an alarm clock and wiring. Schiavo said cellular phone wire was among the contents.

How did a television station manage to cause such chaos? According to newsroom employees at WCMH-TV at the time of this incident, it started out as a routine investigative report. The former inspector general, the reporter and camera crew went to the airport. They shot the piece, packed up and left. They felt good about their report and believed they had accomplished what they had set out to do. Here's where they went wrong: they didn't double check to make sure the bag containing the fake bomb was retrieved and brought back to the station. Later that day, when all the television stations heard on the scanner that a possible bomb was discovered and the airport was being evacuated, all the stations in Columbus—including WCMH-TV—cut into programming and started reporting live. WCMH-TV did not know that the so-called bomb was the same one they had planted earlier in the day. CNN, MSNBC and even the big three networks (on the evening news) began reporting on what was apparently a major security breach at the Columbus Airport.

When WCMH-TV finally figured out what had happened, the red-faced managers huddled to figure out damage control and then immediately began to defend their actions. An investigation was conducted and eventually the television station was cleared of legal wrongdoing because they had actually notified airport security of the investigative report.

Using Hindsight

Hindsight is a tool if used properly. As a news manager, I once worked for Barry Baker, who demanded that each monthly report contain a section titled, "What I would have done differently." It was an exercise to make me think about not making the same mistake twice.

Here are ways you can keep tabs on yourself:

- Keep a spiral notebook.
- Write a daily note about your reporting or producing skills that day.
- Highlight anything that may have gone wrong.
- On the last day of the month look through your notes and see if you would have done anything differently.

It sounds simple, but it works.

Another useful tool is public feedback. But, all too often, news organizations discourage readers, viewers and listeners from participating in the correction process. A 1997 Pew survey found that 70 percent of senior journalists surveyed say news companies do only a fair to poor job of informing the public of errors in reporting. More than half (54 percent) complain that news organizations "lack clear standard operating procedures for handling corrections," and 40 percent say there is no designated person or office at their own news organization for reviewing complaints about mistakes in coverage.

From my years in the news business, I have learned that complaints are a way of life. Many mornings I have come into work and wondered what we did wrong upon discovering 50 messages on my voicemail. Rather than discarding them, I made the effort to listen to them and determine if we had acted irresponsibly. I often call people back if I feel they made a valid point.

If a news manager, reporter or producer who receives a valid complaint would take the time to call the person, explain why a decision was made and suggest a possible remedy, many lawsuits would not be filed.

One warning, however: if you receive a complaint and you realize that it's legitimate and has potential legal ramifications, take the complaint to a manager and let management handle the problem.

If you keep quiet about a major error in judgment and hope it will go away, you may be making yet another mistake, one that will get you deeper in trouble. After all, we now live in a culture of self-accountability.

It wasn't always that way.

We Live in a Different Journalistic Time

The era of the great news prognosticators of the 40s and 50s is long gone, and today's news managers have erected a Berlin Wall between fact reporting and commentary. In today's journalistic climate many look to commentators like Tim Russert or Rush Limbaugh for our political commentary.

For Edward R. Murrow, wielding his journalistic influence was an awesome responsibility.

During World War II, the CBS European broadcast team headed by Murrow represented the conscience of the American people as Hitler, Stalin, and Mussolini grabbed more and more territory in their quest to dominate the world. The team's reports helped this country understand the need to enter the war. Murrow *was* America abroad, and we could not believe our ears when he shared with us the suffering and fear the European people were experiencing. For listeners, Murrow was the common man. We wanted to listen to him and believe. And just as his influence swayed Americans to believe in a war they were reluctant to want, his reports on the Holocaust were equally spellbinding. When he visited one of the camps at Buchenwald, despite his attempt to tone down what he saw, he still presented a powerful picture of the dark side of our humanity.

After the war, Murrow moved into the television medium, at first reluctantly. Radio was his first love and he continued broadcasting in that medium. But he began to see the power of television, and

Edward R. Murrow—Courtesy CBS

he set new standards for what the broadcast news media could accomplish. But though he and William Paley, head of CBS, had been soulmates during the war, fighting a common enemy, that closeness later became strained. Paley felt he had to compromise with the government, the sponsors. Murrow felt, at first, that broadcast news should not be compromised. This would eventually take its toll on Murrow as he tried to straddle both worlds.

As a television journalist, Murrow used his position to challenge the "situations of fear" he saw confronting American society. Possibly his most famous encounter was with the junior Senator from Wisconsin, Joseph McCarthy. Murrow pointed out that the line between investigation and persecution is a fine one. McCarthy felt Murrow had crossed that line. Some say Murrow was partially responsible for McCarthy's downfall. What was certain is that he helped allay some of the fear created by the McCarthy investigations.

History itself is the ultimate dictator of right and wrong. Public perception, many times influenced by the media, will change laws or enhance existing ones. Thus, something that was once right is now wrong. Because of this very pattern, journalists are often chasing their own tails across time. An example is the reporting of the wonders of cocaine in the early 1900s. It was even an ingredient in Coca-Cola. Today journalists report on the drug cartel and addiction problems associated with the same substance, now illegal. Journalism evolves with time and history. It is critical that today's journalist be not only a reporter but also a student of the times in which we live.

CHAPTER 12

You Be the Judge

It may make a difference to all eternity whether we do right or wrong today.

James Freeman Clarke

It's your turn to decide whether the following stories are examples of responsible journalism. First, a story that ended in mid-January 2001, the culmination of the flight of seven heavily armed prison escapees. Four were caught, one committed suicide and the last two were surrounded in a hotel in Colorado. They had no way out and before they gave up, each man wanted five minutes of television time to make a statement. Enter television station KKTV. Here's how the Associated Press covered the story:

> KKTV-TV news anchor Eric Singer spent much of Tuesday night giving viewers updates on the last two Texas prison escapees, who were holed up at an area hotel and talking with police.
>
> Then he became part of the story.
>
> At 11:30 p.m., negotiators told the CBS affiliate that the fugitives wanted to make a statement either on KKTV or a national cable channel before giving up.
>
> Negotiators asked Singer to do the interview—warning him not to upset the convicts—and he did.

"This is the most important story I've ever been a part of," said Singer, 43. "I never in my wildest dreams ever imagined that I would play a role like this." Singer interviewed fugitives Patrick Murphy Jr. and Donald Newbury by telephone for 10 minutes in a live broadcast as part of a deal negotiated by police for the men's surrender.

After the interviews, at about 3:45 a.m. Wednesday, Murphy, a 39-year-old rapist, and Newbury, a 38-year-old convicted robber, walked out of the Holiday Inn and were taken to jail.

The men were among seven inmates who broke out of a maximum-security prison in Kenedy, Texas, on Dec. 13. Four were arrested Monday in nearby Woodland Park. A fifth killed himself as authorities closed in.

Singer, who anchors KKTV's evening newscasts, said the final two fugitives apparently had been watching his station but he doesn't know why they chose him.

Negotiators decided that each fugitive would have five minutes to make a statement and answer questions from Singer. He said an FBI agent sat off-camera and timed the interviews.

"The negotiating team set the stage.... My job was to do the best I could to not exacerbate the situation," Singer said.

Singer said he came up with his own questions but negotiators told him to be careful not to bring up any issues that might anger them. He said he would have liked to have asked the escaped convicts about the chronology after their escape and what happened when they allegedly shot an Irving, Texas police officer.

"But those things were potential hot buttons. Talking about, or having them relive those situations perhaps could have done more harm than good," Singer told NBC's "Today Show."

Did the television station do the right thing? The Associated Press article provides several points of view:

Aly Colon, a media researcher at the Poynter Institute in St. Petersburg, Fla., said broadcasting the interview at the request of either the negotiators or the fugitives raises questions about the news media's independence.

"If you allow outside groups to dictate the manner in which the news is disseminated, it undermines the position of the news media as an evaluator and independent broker of the information," he said.

KKTV news director Brian Rackham said his station decided to air the interview because it might help end the standoff with no loss of life, and because it was an important story.

"I think their (the fugitives') perspective was interesting. We may not agree with it, but it certainly is part of the story," he told Fox News Channel.

Texas prison system spokesman Larry Todd said the negotiators made the right decision to allow the interview.

"Let them have their 15 minutes of fame, because the people watching television know what slime balls they are," Todd said.

Warren Epstein of the *Colorado Springs Gazette* praised the TV anchor, writing:

Ethical issues aside, KKTV did our community a service.

It wasn't just the FBI and local cops who caught the Texas fugitives. It was television, too.

Starting with Fox's "America's Most Wanted," which put the faces out there for a Woodland Park resident to identify, and ending with KKTV/Channel 11 anchor Eric Singer's interviews that led to the surrender, TV played a key role in this tense drama.

I take a lot of shots at TV for its sensationalism, irresponsibility and general trash. But this time they got it right.

Nevertheless, the capture of the remainder of the Texas Seven raised some ethical questions.

It's particularly troubling when a reporter becomes part of a story and when criminals are given high-profile platforms for their grievances.

Bob Steele, an analyst from the Poynter Institute for Media Studies, says there were obviously difficult trade-offs for KKTV to make.

"Clearly there's a risk that in giving a platform to fugitives or terrorists that others may demand such a platform in the future," Steele said. "But that's an unknown consequence."

Actually, I'm not convinced that Patrick Murphy and Donald Newbury really wanted a platform for grievances about the Texas criminal justice system.

Maybe they just wanted to be on television.

In essence, KKTV became involved in the bartering of fame—a dangerous commodity. It seems that every time the media (our newspaper included) make criminals into household names, the allure of infamy becomes that much stronger.

Singer deserves praise, not only for the role he played in the capture but for the poise he showed during his moment in the national limelight.

Let's remember, Singer and KKTV were taking a risk. This whole thing could have turned bad quickly, and if people were killed, there would have been plenty of blame to go around.

Guilty or Not?

There was much talk over the decision of a newspaper in New Bedford, Massachusetts to publish pictures each day of people being arraigned on drug charges. The paper called it "Drug Watch." The publisher took hundreds of phone calls running three to one in favor of the new feature. The publisher felt he had created a true public service, exposing drug pushers, runners and buyers. The ACLU looked at it differently. An ACLU lawyer said it violated journalistic ethics because the paper was showing people who had only been *accused* of crimes. Defense lawyers felt it hindered their client's rights to a fair trial. Every day newspapers and television stations show pictures of people accused of crimes. The question becomes, is this a fair practice? This very question has been debated from the earliest days of the media.

The Ballad of Fugitive Joe

This next story reads like fiction, but it's true. There was a now famous judge in Cambria County, Pennsylvania. His name was Joseph

O'Kicki, and he was tried and convicted of bribery and corruption. O'Kicki contended that he had been framed by the state attorney general, Ernie Preate, and he claimed he had been about to expose the attorney general for the very same charges. O'Kicki was sentenced to the prison into which he had put hundreds of criminals. He contended it was the same as a death sentence.

O'Kicki lived near our television station and stopped by prior to the date he was to report to prison. He said he was not going to prison. I asked him what he meant, and he said, "You'll see." I asked him for an exclusive interview and he declined. I then gave him my card and included my home phone number. The day came when O'Kicki was to report to jail and he was a no-show. The police went to his home, but he was gone. A state-wide manhunt began. It was front-page news across the state.

As the days ticked by, the story started to take on a cult flavor, like the D.B. Cooper manhunt. "O'Kicki sightings" were coming in from three states. There was a media frenzy with reporters being dispatched to check out the leads. The police and FBI set up a command center to handle the calls. Vendors were even selling "Where's Judge Joe" T-shirts. Three months had gone by and the media began to get bored with the story. There was only an occasional story or two as a new fragment of information emerged.

At 5:30 a.m. one Wednesday morning, the phone rang at my home. Like all news directors I feared there had been a breaking story. I grabbed the phone and listened. A woman with broken English said, "Mr. Alan, I have a collect call from Ljubliana, Slovenia, from Father Joe. Will you accept the charge?" I quickly woke up and, sure enough, it was O'Kicki. Where are you? I asked. "I need your help" he replied. I explained that he was a fugitive and I couldn't help him. He asked me questions about the media coverage and if the media had any idea where he was. He told me how he drove to Canada and used a second passport no one knew he had to fly to Germany, where he had a heart attack and was taken in by monks. When he recovered and was well enough to travel he went on to Slovenia, a country which had no extradition treaty with the United States. I asked him if I could interview him by phone and he declined, but he said would think about it and call me back.

What I did next was to confer with my station's general manager. What I did not do was call the authorities and let them know where O'Kicki was. My general manager's eyes lit up when I told him of my early-morning phone call. Like me, he wanted this interview in the worst way. O'Kicki called me almost every day for the next week. He told me stories of how he was framed and about corruption in the highest levels of state government. He finally agreed to a phone interview. In this ten-minute interview he talked only about what he called "his flight to freedom." Our television station made front-page news across the state and other television stations carried the story with our credit. Authorities threatened me for not coming forward with the information. They wanted to know not only about O'Kicki, but also about his wife, Sylvia Onusic, and two children who followed him to Slovenia. My GM, who was very supportive, said he would send a reporter to Slovenia if I could convince O'Kicki to do an on camera interview. I did convince him!

We decided that Donya Archer should be the reporter to go. Marty Ostrow (my general manager) remembers that day:

The reason I felt we needed to send Donya to Slovenia was simple. We needed to put our 10 p.m. news on the "road map." We had just started our newscast and I felt this would show the viewer that we would go to any extreme to deliver the story. Plus, I knew we would get a lot of sampling, which we did. The only one else I spoke to about sending Donya was our libel and slander attorney. I was afraid of the state attorney general arresting us. So, when Donya went to Slovenia, she was on legal grounds, as long as she did not bring him anything that would sustain his hiding.

I made the arrangements with O'Kicki the next day. He requested we bring him supplies like batteries and notepaper. Authorities had issued an arrest warrant for O'Kicki's wife for aiding and abetting. I didn't want the same thing happening to us. I let him know we could not comply with his request. The day before Donya was to leave, the children's grandmother came to the television station (having been called by O'Kicki) with a box of gifts for the kids including two big stuffed rabbits. Crying, she pleaded with me to take them to her grandchildren. Donya packed them away and off she went. No one at the television station knew what was happening and believed Donya was on vacation. Donya recalls her adventure:

Donya Archer with Judge Joe O'Kicki in Slovenia—Courtesy Donya Archer

April 28, 1993, I arrived in the recovering war-torn nation of Slovenia, armed with a couple VHS camcorders, an English-Slovenian dictionary, and the hope that this wily fugitive wouldn't stand me up. In the weeks prior to my journey, we'd set up a place to meet in Ljubliana and an itinerary—but it was all a gamble. We had no assurance he was even living in Ljubliana. However, O'Kicki was true to his word. Dressed like a dandy in a suit and hat, he met me in the lobby of my hotel, not a minute late. He was craving the opportunity to tell his story and show his enemies his charmed life as a free man in Europe.

O'Kicki was already a bit of a celebrity in Ljubliana. The local papers were tipped to his story via the Associated Press. As a result, I had a reporter from the magazine *Mladina* pestering me for more on his story. So I agreed to let him sit in on my interviews with O'Kicki, if he would serve as my translator when I interviewed Slovene authorities. For three days, I interviewed O'Kicki in various locations throughout Ljubliana. I was never able to sleuth out where he lived, but he walked the streets proudly, taking in an afternoon opera, sipping espresso in the cafes. It was a far cry from the life he was sentenced to live at Western Penitentiary.

In the course of our interviews, O'Kicki rehashed his case and pointed the finger at his powerful enemies in Pennsylvania. He believed his two- to five-year prison sentence was a death sentence, because he would have to live beside many criminals he'd sentenced during his years on the bench. He also told me he had cancer and feared he would not live to see his release. To me, he looked quite healthy. I had spent weeks compiling and memorizing information on his trial and the evidence against him, so that I would be able to counter his allegations of gross misconduct. I wanted the reports to be a fair depiction of his plight, not a forum for a convicted criminal. Because both of O'Kicki's parents were native Slovenians, O'Kicki was considered a Slovene citizen. At the time, under Slovene law, he could not be extradited.

In Western Pennsylvania, the search for O'Kicki was front-page news, and authorities, including Pennsylvania's attorney general Ernie Preate, assured the press they were doing everything they could to bring him to justice. However, when I talked to the head of Slovenia's version of the F.B.I., I got a different story. He assured me he had *not* been contacted by Interpol, the FBI, or Mr. Preate's office. The only call

he'd gotten regarding O'Kicki was from the Cambria County Sheriff's Office. O'Kicki's retort: Pennsylvania authorities didn't want him back because he knew too much about them.

Donya returned through London where she dubbed her interview tapes and overnighted them back to the station. They arrived a day before she did. We were afraid her tapes would be seized by the State Department at the airport. Meanwhile, I was tipped off that the state police were seeking a search warrant to remove the interview tapes from the station and an injunction to prevent them from airing. Acting on this information I contacted the National Association of Broadcasters (NAB). Their First Amendment lawyer called the state attorney general and informed him he could not get such an injunction. I then notified the state police that we already had the tapes and there were copies at several locations and a search warrant would be useless. We then met Donya when she returned to Pittsburgh. The station aired a ten-part interview with "Fugitive Joe," as people were now calling him. Each day the transcript of the previous night's installment was printed on the front page of several newspapers. We made best-effort attempts to air opposing viewpoints to O'Kicki's revelations, but seldom did anyone want to comment.

Other media accused me of paying O'Kicki for the interview, but I did not.

An interesting sidenote to our involvement in the O'Kicki story: O'Kicki mentioned that he was writing a book on his experiences, one that would finally expose the crimes of his enemies. Six months after our interview aired, I received a large sealed envelope from the judge. He said it was proof of his innocence and would "bring down state government." I was instructed not to open it and to forward it the the FBI. I did just that. Shortly thereafter, federal corruption charges targeted state attorney general Ernie Preate. He was accused of a felony involving campaign finance wrongdoing. He resigned from office in 1995, was convicted and subsequently served nearly a year in federal prison. I will never know if the two events were related, or if the envelope I delivered was indeed the much-talked-about O'Kicki book.

Judge O'Kicki died in December of 1996. His wife returned to Cambria County to face the charges against her in 1998. Dennis Roddy of the *Pittsburgh Post-Gazette* reported the final event in the O'Kicki Saga:

EBENSBURG, Pa.—Sylvia Onusic, widow of Judge Joseph O'Kicki, the renowned jurist, moocher and international fugitive, was out from under the cloud. Criminal charges that prevented her from coming home from Slovenia were gone.

"Are you happy it's over?" someone asked.

She said nothing.

"Any reaction?"

Silence.

Onusic, back from the medieval city where her husband died in exile, returned solely to resolve some criminal charges. Questions? Stick 'em in your ear....

In the marble columned courtroom where a decade earlier her husband was invested as president judge amid fanfares by 10 trumpeters rented for the occasion, Sylvia Onusic was accepted without musical accompaniment into the Accelerated Rehabilitative Disposition program for first offenders.

The O'Kicki saga, with tales of payoffs given, bribes demanded, bankers squeezed, and underwear exposed, was the greatest entertainment in Cambria County since public hangings were discontinued.

But that was five years ago. This time, a half-dozen reporters snoozed through the hearing, then left when Sylvia wouldn't talk.

Even Gerry Long, the judge who had just made Onusic a footnote in the picaresque legend of Fugitive Joe, wasn't satisfied. He was one of those against whom Joe had vowed a deep and solemn revenge, and now here he was, giving the guy's widow a break. Long had bitten hard into the bonbon of criminal scandal and had yet to find its creamy nougat center.

"I just wonder if he's really dead," Long shrugged.

O'Kicki, imperious, ruthless and brilliant, died in Ljubljana, Dec. 2, 1996, but many in this town say they'll believe it when they see the body, preferably with a wooden stake protruding.

The truth about Joe O'Kicki may never be known. But his story raises several questions about the nature of responsible journalism.

- Was it right not to notify the authorities of O'Kicki's whereabouts?
- Was it right to take the grandmother's gifts to his children?
- Was it right to air O'Kicki's accusations?
- Was it right for a television station to become part of this story?

CHAPTER 13

The Responsibility Test

I've always wanted responsibility because I want the power responsibility brings.

Sam Rayburn

Here's your chance to assess your own level of journalistic responsibility. This test was created by Michelle Betz of the University of Central Florida, with help from George Bagley and Lisa Mills, also of the University of Central Florida's Nicholson School of Journalism, along with Robin Chapman.

The test simply requires you to read each question and select an answer. In order for the test to be accurate, you must answer honestly! You can see how you score at the end of the chapter.

Get a pencil and a piece of paper and see how you do. Pass this test along and see how others in your newsroom or class do. If you're about to enter the business, this test may be a valuable tool. If you're a working journalist, we hope this test will make you think. You may also want to retake this test a year from now and see if you score differently.

The Test

1. It's 4:55 p.m. in the northeastern United States and you're getting ready for the 6:00 p.m. newscast. You're on the

assignment desk at a local affiliate and hear on the scanner that two people have been found dead in their home. You dispatch the live truck and a crew. The reporter arrives on the scene, sees all the usual—police cars, yellow tape, etc. The other three stations are also there. At about 5:20 p.m., the police officers come out and inform the media that it's an elderly couple who committed suicide in their car in their garage. How do you cover the story?

a) You do a live report from the scene and report the couple's names.
b) You don't cover the story at all.
c) The story is mentioned in the 6:00 p.m. newscast as a script story.
d) You do a voiceover.

2. An individual has been leaking information to you for several years and has always been reliable. However, she now tells you a story about corruption that could bring down the county administration if it's true. What do you do?

a) You discuss the story with your colleagues, then decide it isn't worth doing.
b) Your producer and news director want to know who your source is before you do the story. You refuse to tell them and so you can't do the story.
c) You report the story right away; after all, your source is credible.
d) You don't report the story until you can verify the information.

3. Your station is in the middle of doing a story that is critical of a major sports organization. At the same time, your station covers a major sporting event and one of the sponsors is the organization that you're examining. That organization has supplied caps with their logo to all media. What do you do?

a) You take a cap and wear it.
b) You decide to kill the story.

c) You continue to do the story but it's much less critical than when it started.

d) You do the story as planned and make sure it airs. You don't take a cap.

4. You are an intern in a newsroom. A new restaurant that is set to have its grand opening the next day has just sent over bucketfuls of food for everyone in the newsroom. As you help the producer line up that evening's show, you see that there is a voiceover about that restaurant. You're curious so you pull the script and see that it's a very complimentary story that to you sounds more like a commercial than a news story. What do you do?

a) You say nothing. After all, you're just an intern.

b) You mention it to another intern who says, "What's the big deal?"

c) You ask the producer if doing the story is ethical in light of the fact that the restaurant has just sent over a pile of food.

d) You suggest to the producer that it may not be such a good idea to run the story.

5. You are assigned to cover the lead story for your 11 p.m. newscast. It isn't just the biggest story of the day; it's the biggest story of the year. You've been at the courthouse all evening interviewing the principals and your package is edited and has been transmitted back to the station and is ready to air by 10:15 p.m. At 10:20 p.m. your crew tells you that while attempting to move the live truck to a better signal, they accidentally raised the mast into a metal cross-bar from a nearby streetlight and they can no longer transmit a live report. All the other live trucks belonging to the station are on assignment and cannot get to your location in time. All your competitors will be going live with this earth-shaking story, but you cannot. The assignment desk tells you to tape an opening and closing stand-up for your report at the courthouse designed to "look live." They tell you to open with "Thanks, Steve [your anchor's name]. It has been a momen-

tous day...," and end with, "I'm Jennie Smith, reporting from the courthouse. Now back to you, Steve, in the studio." What do you do?

   a) You do a live phoner.
   b) You do as the desk asks.
   c) You ask to return to the newsroom so you can do a live debrief from set.
   d) You don't file anything.

6. You are taping a routine stand-up at the White House on an ordinary day that so far has produced very little news. Your report involves a presidential visit to a local school. As you set up for your shoot, your videographer has a microphone coiled on the grass adjacent to the spot from which a colleague from a competing station is also taping a stand-up. The other reporter is out of earshot, but because of the microphone on the ground you hear in your earpiece what the reporter is saying. You learn that the reporter's story includes the extraordinary news that the president's chief-of-staff is about to be fired for having an affair with a White House intern. The competing station's newscast will begin 30 minutes later in the day than your own due to a football game. What do you do?

   a) You check out the story and try to confirm it. If you can't confirm it, you don't run it.
   b) You run with the story.
   c) You don't run anything.
   d) You speak to the colleague from the other station, tell her what you heard and that you plan to run the story as well.

7. The names of rape victims in your state are a matter of public record but are not used in news reports. It is an unwritten understanding among prosecutors, the police and the news media that this particular type of crime is of a nature that broadcasting the name of a victim could devastate a person's life and could, in fact, discourage other victims from coming forward, thus inhibiting prosecutors from convicting many other perpetrators. One of your city's most prominent

women becomes the victim of a brutal rape. You and other members of the media know her name but conceal her identity. On the eve of the trial of the man accused of the assault you learn that a colleague at a competing news organization plans to reveal the victim's name in a report that night. At that point the victim's name will be common knowledge in your city and any pretense of confidentiality will be ended. What do you do?

a) You contact the competing station and try to convince them not to identify the woman.
b) You identify the woman.
c) You do not identify the woman.
d) You ask the news director what to do.

8. You are covering a story in which a local woman, after a bitter divorce, is accusing her ex-husband of molesting their three-and-a-half-year-old daughter. Both the mother and the father are prominent surgeons with excellent reputations. The judge has held closed hearings on the case in family court, has sealed the records, and has ordered the woman to produce the child for visitations with the father. The woman refuses and is sent to jail in contempt of court, where she has become a national symbol of a mother ferociously defending her battered child. Someone leaks copies of the sealed court testimony to all the members of the local media. The testimony is ambiguous. Three experts who interviewed the child say the child was horribly molested, and the details they cite are graphic. Two other experts, who also interviewed the child, testify there is absolutely no evidence of any molestation. There is no corroborative physical evidence in the records that you have. Anyone using the sealed testimony faces a contempt of court citation. But since the information has been leaked to all the local media, there is very little chance you would be prosecuted for using the material. You receive the material at noon. The story is the lead story at 6:00 p.m. What do you do?

a) You run with it.
b) You call the court and ask them if they will unseal the records so you can use them.

c) You try to contact other sources to get corroboration, thereby allowing you to report the information from sources other than the court documentation.

d) You don't report the information.

9. You write three humorous columns a week for a local paper and have been doing so for the past 10 years. You are one of the most popular columnists at the paper. One week your child is in the hospital, your wife has left you for the sports editor, your Visa and American Express cards have just been canceled for late payment, and you have just returned from visiting your 85-year-old mother who is dying of cancer. You have one hour to write your regular Friday column and you have never missed a deadline. You are depressed and in despair and you have no ideas for a funny column. What do you do?

a) You tell your editor about your situation and you don't write anything.

b) You write a non-humorous column.

c) You find a column written by a colleague in another state 15 years ago and you use the idea, changing the names and location to fit your city.

d) You don't write anything at all.

10. It is a cold, cloudy day in a big city in the eastern United States. The forecast is for snow which, when it does hit the city a few times a year, snarls traffic during rush hour. During the day you are assigned to cover the "snow preparation" story, doing interviews with the appropriate public officials, and shooting video of people buying snow shovels, and showing some snow removal equipment being prepared for use. You prepare your report and also throw in some video of the previous snowstorm and the accidents it caused. Your report is scheduled to be the lead story on the station's 6:00 p.m. newscast. At 5:15 p.m. the newsroom gets a call from a viewer in a suburb 10 miles north of the city that the snow is beginning to fall very lightly. The news director assigns you and a crew to take a live truck and "drive till you find snow," with the understanding that you will then set up the live shot

and front your pre-packaged report from this unknown location where it has now, reportedly, begun to snow. As you leave the station's parking lot it is 5:25 p.m. and the streets around you are clogged with rush-hour traffic. You realize that even giving your crew a minimum of 10 minutes to set up the live shot, lights and camera you now have barely 25 minutes to "drive till you find snow." It takes you eight minutes to inch up the street to the first light. The videographer driving the car, also aware of the impending deadline, tells you he knows of a side street nearby where there is a large pile of unmelted snow from the last storm which could be used as a backdrop for your live report. He suggests you drive there immediately and begin setting up your live shot. He points out that since it is dark, no one will know the difference and based on the time of night, the traffic and the vague location of the "snow" you have been assigned to "drive to" you have no other practical choices. What do you do?

a) You return to the station and don't go live.
b) You report from the videographer's position and do a live shot, reporting that there is no snow.
c) You continue to look for real snow.
d) You do as the cameraman suggests.

11. A new president is being inaugurated after a controversial and bitter campaign. Half a million people have turned out on the streets of Washington for the inaugural parade. 500 people have gathered near the Lincoln Memorial to protest the inauguration and you are assigned to cover the protest. When you arrive, the crowd is milling around talking and drinking coffee. By the time you have set up the camera they have begun to chant slogans against the new administration and you roll tape, getting some good pictures of the demonstration. You shoot video for 15 minutes, during which time 20 of the demonstrators get into a fight with police and two police officers are injured and taken away by ambulance. Fifty demonstrators are arrested and taken away in patrol cars. Your videographer takes the camera off the tripod while you call the station with the information. Both of you go into the news truck because it's cold. As you talk on the phone,

you look outside the window of the truck and notice that since you ceased taping, the demonstrators have returned to milling around and drinking coffee. What do you do?

   a) You find another location that's easier to report on.
   b) You file your original report on the demonstration.
   c) You do not file anything.
   d) You get pictures of the stillness, the demonstrations and the arrests and report all of it.

12. You work in a medium-sized market in the south-eastern United States. You are producing a 10:00 p.m. news-cast on a weeknight. Generally, your executive producer prefers that you focus on local news in the first block of the show, and then concentrate on national and international news after the first commercial break. Your lead story will be a live shot from the scene of an accident in which a train hit a car full of teenagers. Eyewitnesses say the teenage driver ig-nored the warning lights at the crossing and pulled around the gates after they had been lowered. Your reporter phones you and says she has "great stuff…sound bites with witness-es, an interview with the shaken train engineer, and video of four bodies lying near the tracks covered with yellow police tarps." After you hang up with the reporter, your tape editor informs you that new video has just come down the feed from India. There has just been an earthquake in a rural region of that nation. The video contains graphic video of uncovered bodies being pulled from the rubble. As you stack your show, which of the following decisions would you make?

   a) You show the video of the bodies in both cases.
   b) You show the video of the covered bodies on the local story, but not the uncovered bodies from India.
   c) You do not show either of the videos of bodies.
   d) You show the video of the uncovered bodies from India, but not the covered bodies on the local story.

13. You work in a medium-sized market in the south-western United States. You are producing an 11:00 p.m. news-cast on a weeknight. You only have one reporter-videographer

team working. They are assigned to go to a home in a working class neighborhood where law enforcement officials believe there has been a home invasion/murder. The victim is a male in his mid-thirties. Your team gets interviews with law enforcement, reaction sound bites from neighbors, and video of the crime scene. You decide you must lead with this story as a live shot. At 10:55 p.m. your reporter calls you to say police now believe this is a suicide. What do you do?

  a) You lead with the live shot, but have the reporter explain this "latest development" right off the top. You do not run any of the video or sound bites she collected.
  b) You lead with the live shot and package, having the reporter explain this "latest development" in her live tag after the package.
  c) You drop the reporter live shot, but run an anchor voiceover of the incident.
  d) You drop the story altogether and begin your newscast with story two.

14. You are a reporter out of town on assignment for your television news station. The story needs some man-on-the-street shots of people shopping. It is a weekday morning, not many shoppers are out, and you are about to give up when you spot a local mall. You know there are likely to be a few shoppers there, and you could get at least a couple of sound bites. On the other hand, you know that if mall security spots you they will insist that you get prior permission from mall management before shooting. You and your videographer have only ninety minutes before catching your flight back home, and you know from experience that you would be lucky to get permission in your limited time frame were you to ask. Since this is your only opportunity to get your local sound, what do you do?

  a) You go directly to mall management for permission anyway and hope for the best. You realize that it will take time and if you don't get permission you likely will not get any shots.

b) You stand outside the mall entrance on a public side-walk and hope to interview people as they enter or leave the mall.

c) You go into the mall and record your man-on-the-street shots until mall management kicks you out, then use the sound you were lucky enough to record.

d) You eliminate the man-on-the-street sound bits and do the best with what you have.

15. While covering a spot news story about a little girl recovering from a swimming pool accident you await your final shot: the girl being loaded onto a med-evac chopper for transport to the local hospital. While waiting, you notice a line of neighbors and family members lining themselves up to form a human wall between your photographer and the little girl as she is rolled across the parking lot on the gurney. The shot is critical and you know you are in trouble if you do not get it. What do you do?

a) You tell the other videographer on the scene to set himself up in an obvious position to draw attention so the "wall" thinks he's the shooter, then you put your original videographer on the other side to get the good shots.

b) You shoot a wide-shot of the wall and make note of it in the story's narration.

c) Before the girl is evacuated, you step over to the friends and family members and try to negotiate with them.

d) You forgo the shot; it is not worth hassling with the locals.

Scoring

Each question earns you a score from 1 to 4 points.

1.	a-1	b-4	c-3	d-2
2.	a-2	b-3	c-1	d-4
3.	a-2	b-1	c-3	d-4
4.	a-1	b-2	c-3	d-4
5.	a-3	b-2	c-4	d-1
6.	a-4	b-1	c-2	d-3
7.	a-3	b-1	c-4	d-2
8.	a-1	b-2	c-4	d-3
9.	a-4	b-3	c-1	d-2
10.	a-3	b-4	c-2	d-1
11.	a-2	b-3	c-1	d-4
12.	a-1	b-3	c-4	d-2
13.	a-2	b-1	c-3	d-4
14.	a-3	b-4	c-1	d-2
15.	a-1	b-4	c-2	d-3

If your total score is:

50–60 Congratulations! Despite the daily pressures from management and the competition, you manage to do your job responsibly.

40–49 You are doing quite well in the area of responsibility, but you are succumbing to the pressures of competition.

30–39 You are following the pack and as a result your level of responsibility is suffering.

15–29 You absolutely must examine what you do as journalist and how you do it. You definitely need to strive to be more responsible.

CHAPTER 14

Election Night 2000

I know nothing grander, better exercise, better digestion, more positive proof of the past, the triumphant result of faith in humankind, than a well-contested American national election.

Walt Whitman

Sweeping Up the Mess

For months we reported wide swings in the polls. George Bush was ahead one day and Al Gore the next, so was it really a surprise that election night went so badly? And it all happened during the November sweeps period, forcing most newsrooms in America to change front pages and change lead broadcast stories to keep up with the presidential election court fight of the day.

The roots of modern election coverage in the United States—and, for that matter, the birth of broadcast news itself—began on election night, November 2, 1920, with the Harding-Cox presidential race. The Associated Press gathered the results from the election and provided them to KDKA radio in Pittsburgh, which aired the news. Eighty years later that sequence of news reporting remains true, but broadcast technology and techniques have changed. In 1920, there were no rules, no basic tenets for on-air reporting, and no guidelines for the newcomers to the business. But no matter how many rules and policies news organizations have put in place since then, much can

Courtesy Columbia Journalism Review

still go wrong. It was never more apparent than when the news media reported what happened on election night, November 7, 2000.

As the night progressed it became apparent that Florida would have the final say as to who the next president would be. All the networks except ABC announced that Al Gore had won Florida while the polls were still open in the panhandle, not realizing there are two time zones in the Sunshine State. When more votes were going

Courtesy CNN

George W.'s way, the networks backpedaled and placed Florida in the "too close to call" category. Then at about 1:15 a.m. Eastern Time the networks declared George W. Bush the new president of the United States. Not so fast—when the vote totals narrowed in South Florida, the networks reversed again, leaving America dazed and confused.

The next day, when NBC's Tom Brokaw was asked if he had egg on his face, he replied, "No, an omelet." Dan Rather called for a uniform poll closing time nationwide.

Peter Jennings offered this observation in his daily e-mail for November 8:

Well, this is a mess, isn't it? And some of it clearly of our making. We were one of those news organizations that, in our election projection last night, gave Florida to Al Gore, took it away, gave it to George W. Bush and then took it away, to leave it where it is today: too close to call. Currently Mr. Bush is slightly ahead in Florida's popular vote, but they are so close (1,784 votes out of almost 6 million total) that Florida law requires the vote to be recounted.

As for what so many news organizations did last night, including us...we are flawed, and the process by which we have for many years now estimated the vote and projected the results is imperfect. We make projections based on mathematical models—and in such an unpredictable election, as it turned out to be, we should have stayed our hand. Why didn't we? (All of us, that is.) Because we and the political establishment, and to some extent millions of voters who want results in a hurry, have become invested in a process that has provided very precise guidelines for more than 15 years. Some of us, myself included, long for the old days when we stayed on until every last vote was counted. We do not live in those times anymore, and as embarrassed as we are today, we look forward to a debate on how the system can be realistically improved. One point on closing times: Gov. Jeb Bush of Florida (candidate Bush's brother) said today that some news organizations called Florida before all the polls were closed there. We did not.

A congressman from Mississippi called for hearings on Capital Hill. The networks responded, and CNN put together an independent panel to review what had happened. Meanwhile, the *San Francisco Chronicle* reported:

The head of CBS News has accepted blame for erroneously predicting victory in Florida for Vice President Al Gore on election night and then calling the entire contest for Gov. George W. Bush, explaining that the decisions were based on bad information from exit polls and a computer malfunction in one county. "We were as good as the information we were getting from sources we trusted, " CBS News President Andrew Heyward said in a letter to Rep. W.J. "Billy" Tauzin, R-La., chairman of the House Commerce Committee's telecommunications panel. "In this case, that information was not good, and neither were we." Heyward said that his network's initial call for Gore at 7:50 p.m. EST on Nov. 7 was based on Voter News Service exit polls and actual vote data, interpreted through tested statistical models. Heyward's letter, as well as letters from five other news outlets, was released Tuesday by Tauzin's office. The congressman wrote to the organizations after the election, saying he was "greatly dismayed" by their misleading calls and requesting detailed responses. Heyward's letter was by far the most explicit in suggesting causes.

The networks are conducting their own investigations into the fiasco, although none has been completed. On election night, CBS, NBC, ABC, CNN, Fox and The Associated Press all projected that Gore had won Florida around 8 p.m. EST. Later, all six news outlets took back the projection.

Two weeks later, after the Florida election was certified for George W. Bush, he immediately proclaimed victory while Al Gore filed a lawsuit to contest the election. Citizens of Florida filed over 40 local lawsuits and there was still no closure to one of the closest presidential elections ever.

During the third week of turmoil, according to Elizabeth Jensen of the *Los Angeles Times*, ABC completed an internal review of exactly what happened on election night:

Based on a preliminary review of its election night miscalls, ABC News blamed competitive pressures and bad exit poll information and released guidelines Friday for future elections that the network said would correct some of the problems. One change ABC plans is not letting the employees making projections see a television set, so they won't know what their rivals are doing. Like other networks, ABC incorrectly projected the outcome of the presidential vote in Florida twice, ultimately declaring Texas Gov. George W. Bush the president-elect, before backtracking and deciding the state was too close to call. Fox News Channel was the first to declare Bush the winner, while ABC was the last of the major TV news outlets to do so. The bad projections are expected to be the subject of congressional hearings early next year. The projections were based partly on exit poll information from Voter News Service, a consortium of networks and the Associated Press. The errors made on election night were the "result of a combination of errors in the data provided by the Voter News Service and the inappropriate reaction to competitive pressures" said ABC News resident David Westin. Westin said although the ABC News decision desk is separate from the control room and newsroom, employees have been able to "see who's calling what, when. It's understandable why they're curious," he said, but ABC needs to have its projections "uncontaminated by competitive pressures." Westin said no personnel will be reprimanded for the election night problems, noting, "These were honest mistakes...and they were humbling to all of us." Other changes ABC announced include not projecting the winner of any state until all of the state's polls are closed. In the past, ABC News, like competing networks, has pledged only to refrain from projecting a state's winner until the vast majority of the state's polls have closed. ABC will also make it more clear that it is only making projections. Over the years, Westin said, "We've fallen into the trap of using short-form in describing our projections. In fact, a projection is not the calling of a race. " Finally, ABC will support appointment of an outside expert to review Voter News Service. "Clearly, there were data problems," Westin said, adding that he believes ABC News is better off devoting resources to making Voter News Service "the best it can be" than funding a competing polling operation, as some have suggested.

What this all boils down to is that prior to the election, in a cost cutting move, the networks and the Associated Press had formed a joint venture called the Voter News Service (VNS), resulting in the loss of autonomy. Thus, they all ended up making the same wrong turn while projecting the winner.

Nearly a month after the election the Federal Communications Commission became involved, and was asked to investigate four major U.S. television networks for awarding Florida to Democrat Al Gore before the polls closed in the state on election day. Smithwick & Belendiuk, a small law firm that represents radio, television, telephone and other communications clients before the FCC, filed a five-page complaint against the ABC, NBC, CBS and Fox networks questioning whether they had subverted the public interest in making their election calls. Some U.S. lawmakers have even said the announcement by the networks about Florida may have led some Americans to skip voting. "Something went wrong. Let's find out what that something is and let's fix it," Arthur Belendiuk, one of the firm's founders, told Reuters in an interview.

As new information came to the forefront of the investigation, it was revealed that a cousin of George W. Bush was on the "Decision Desk" at Fox, the first to call Florida for Al Gore. This brought up ethical questions, as the Associated Press reported:

"There should be a red team and a blue team. The reason everyone was in the same boat was cost. We're going to have to bite the bullet and spend a little more money," [Fox News president Roger] Ailes said. Fox paid $2 million this year to be part of VNS.

Fox is starting to talk to other television and print organizations about a possible partnership. Many journalists were skeptical about Fox's announcement, dismissing it as damage control from the network that had George W. Bush's first cousin John Ellis heading its election decision desk. After Ellis recommended calling Florida for the Texas governor, Fox became the first network to declare Bush the presidential winner.

"If I had my [heinie] hanging out there with Ellis running my decision desk, I'd be announcing I was canceling VNS, too," joked one exec.

While Fox said it had launched an internal investigation of Ellis's role—which was criticized even by Fox talk show host Bill O'Reilly—yesterday Ailes sang a different song, saying that Ellis "called it for Bush at 2 in the morning, and it was upheld" by Florida's official certification.

As for Ellis calling Florida for Al Gore earlier in the evening, "he was sitting there at 7:50 saying, 'These models look wrong.' Competitive pressure [from the other networks] made us go, too. It was a mistake," said [Ailes].

By the end of November, a Washington watchdog group had asked federal antitrust authorities to break up the Voter News Service. In a November 27 letter to the Federal Trade Commission and the Department of Justice, the American Antitrust Institute attributed the gaffes to the major news operations all having relied on the same numbers for their calls. "The Voter News Service fiasco makes us wonder whether things have already arrived at the point where a mistake or bias will not be corrected by the normal give and take of competition among media firms," the group said. VNS declined comment.

By the beginning of December, a bill was already put before Congress which called for a universal poll closing time nationwide. Maybe someone heard Dan Rather? This report ran on December 6 in *Broadcasting & Cable*:

Rep. Edward Markey (D-Mass.) introduced a bill that would require polls in all states to close at the same time. "We have an opportunity now to rectify this situation, establish a uniform poll closing time, and minimize the potential that future premature projections by the television networks regarding the winners of a presidential election will influence voter behavior in other states," Markey said. The bill, as Markey introduced it, would close nationwide polls at 9 p.m. Eastern Standard time. So polls would close in the central time zone at 8 p.m. and in the mountain time zone at 7 p.m. The new law would require states in the western time zone to delay the change to daylight savings time for two weeks so polls there would also close at 7 p.m. But Markey says he is open to considering other ideas, such as a 24-hour polling period with a uniform closing time, or a 10 p.m. EST close.

More Confusion

The final blow for Al Gore came on the night of December 12. Just hours before the deadline for appointing the electors, in a 5-4 opinion, the United States Supreme Court effectively made George W. Bush the next president of the United States. Just after 10 p.m. Eastern Time, reporters ran from the courthouse and attempted to convey a confusing decision from a deeply divided court. The situation quickly became another media circus. Howard Kurtz of the *Washington Post* reviewed how the networks handled that now famous night in American history:

Network journalists had waited through an interminably long day for the U.S. Supreme Court to settle the presidential election, and when the decision finally came...no one was quite sure what it meant.

What followed was another extraordinary, ultimately riveting evening of television—one among too many to recall over the past month, and perhaps the last in this long, strange election saga. Correspondents, anchors, pundits and scholars struggled to understand what the court had said, and officials of the two campaigns struggled to understand what the justices—and the talking heads on television—were trying to tell them.

Courtesy the Associated Press

For nearly half an hour after 10 p.m., the correspondents stood shivering in the cold outside the marble building, reading passages as they spoke to millions of viewers, pondering questions aloud, finally fumbling their way to the conclusion that George W. Bush had all but won the presidency.

At least, they were pretty sure. That's what it sounded like. But there were these six separate opinions. It took precious minutes just to figure out that this was essentially a 5 to 4 ruling against Al Gore.

"We are in the midst of trying to sort this out and clarify exactly what the court has done," ABC's Peter Jennings said. "It is, quite frankly, not particularly easy." "What's not clear to me at this point, Dan, is what is the remedy when they remand it back to the Florida Supreme Court," CBS's Bob Schieffer said from beneath a woolen cap. "There's just no way the court thinks a recount is possible," said NBC's Pete Williams. But ABC's Terry Moran cautioned that "there may be some light left here...for Al Gore."

This was journalism on the run, a deep-freeze legal seminar, a national group grope so tentative that the networks weren't quite sure what headline to throw on the screen. After a day in which some talking heads spoke about whether the justices were moving away from a 5 to 4 ruling because they were taking so long to decide (although it was lightning speed by Supreme standards), was this...it? Had the 35-day mini-series come to an end?

What threw the assembled anchors and reporters was that the Supreme Court was sending the case back to Florida's high court, leaving at least the theoretical possibility that the maneuvering might drag on. And that seven justices expressed concern about the constitutionality of the recount the Florida court had dramatically ordered just last Friday, which seemed an eternity ago. "A lot of people are sitting at home saying, 'Who's winning, Bush or Gore?'" Jennings observed. "I believe, from everything I've heard, Bush," George Stephanopoulos replied. "You could still have a fight here over which slate is going to be in," added ABC's Jack Ford.

"How the Florida Supreme Court interprets it, we just don't know yet," said CNN's Roger Cossack. But as they called their campaign sources and checked the news wires, the journalists grew a bit more certain in their pronouncements.

"It's an all-out victory for the Bush team, no matter why," said NBC's Dan Abrams.

"This election is over," said ABC's Ford. "I make no claim to being a legal expert," said CNN's Jeff Greenfield, "but it sure sounds to me that the court left no room for the Florida Supreme Court to construct a recount." "It does appear this election has come to an end," declared NBC's Tim Russert. He added that "it's extremely difficult to accept defeat, no doubt about it. But Al Gore will accept this verdict from the Supreme Court."

Schieffer noted a dissent in which Justice John Paul Stevens said the country would never know who won the election. "If that doesn't throw a cloud over the election, I don't know what does," the CBS newsman said.

Harvard's Laurence Tribe, a Gore lawyer, would not wave the white flag, saying gamely it was "not impossible" that the case would make it back for a third Supreme Court hearing. But NBC's Tom Brokaw wasn't buying Tribe's argument.

"With all due respect," Brokaw said, "it does sound like a bit of a reach to me."

By 10:57, nearly an hour after the story broke, Democratic National Committee Chairman Ed Rendell, a staunch Gore loyalist, flatly predicted that the vice president would not fight on. "I think he will concede, Tom," he told Brokaw.

Gore conceded and Bush was our new president. News organizations vowed to go to Florida and count the ballots on their own under the Freedom of Information Act. The networks had to regroup and ordered investigations into the Voter News Service and their own actions, and prepared for what was sure to be a cloud of controversy.

The Investigation

The election officially ended the night of December 12, 2000. Al Gore, in what many called the "speech of his life," conceded the election and called for a united nation. An hour later George W. Bush gave a toned-down victory speech, also asking the nation to put aside its differences.

Despite a gracious concession speech, there was still division in both political and public arenas. The Reverend Jesse Jackson proclaimed that George W. Bush was crowned, not elected. Some Florida voters were still convinced that their votes may not have been counted. News agencies and citizens rights groups moved in and filed Freedom of Information Act requests to have the ballots finally counted. Meanwhile, the discussion about what the television and radio networks had done on election night continued.

The day George W. became the president-elect, Rep. Billy Tauzin (R-La.) assured the news networks that he was not assuming their coverage on election night was biased, but he was investigating it just the same. In letters to CBS News president Andrew Heyward, NBC president Bob Wright, ABC News president David Westin, Fox News president Roger Ailes and CNN president Tom Johnson, Tauzin thanked the executives for assuring him that their coverage was straightforward, then went on to state why the issue was still under investigation. "Our own analysis of the networks' election night 'victory calls' indicates an incontrovertible bias in the results that were reported." Tauzin then listed several examples showing that the networks more readily called close states for Gore than for Bush. "In short, the data collection system and models used by the networks produced results which consistently reported Vice President Gore's victories earlier than Governor Bush's victories, portraying a skewed electoral picture and disenfranchising many American voters. By any definition of the word, isn't that bias?" Tauzin also assured the network heads that he would be "mindful of your First Amendment rights and protections in this matter." Hearings were then scheduled for mid-February.

The Congressional Hearing

On February 14, 2001, in a room on Capital Hill, all the network news presidents assembled to explain to a congressional panel just what had gone wrong on election night. The *Washington Post*'s Howard Kurtz reported on the proceedings:

Forced to relive their Election Day nightmare in a high-ceilinged House hearing room, television's top news executives admitted yesterday what the whole world already knows: that they screwed up royally by twice blowing their projections of the presidential vote in Florida.

Courtesy CNN

"Our Florida flip-flops are deeply embarrassing to us," said CBS News President Andrew Heyward.

"We let our viewers down," said Fox News President Roger Ailes.

"Make no mistake about it, we are embarrassed by those errors," said NBC News President Andrew Lack.

But Ailes challenged Rep. Billy Tauzin (R-La.), chairman of the House Energy and Commerce Committee, over his "adversarial" approach, saying he resented having "to take an oath as if we have something to hide. We do not."

First, though, the executives had to cool their heels for five hours, part of which was devoted to more than 25 members of Congress scoring political points and venting about the election.

Tauzin said the networks' exit poll model contained "statistical biases in favor of Democrats...and against Republicans," although he allowed that there was "no evidence of intentional bias." But Rep. Ed Markey (D-Mass.) dismissed as "preposterous" suggestions of a "vast left-wing conspiracy."

Rep. Henry Waxman (D-Calif.) chastised Fox News Channel for employing George W. Bush's first cousin, John Ellis, whose 2:16 a.m. projection in Florida "created a presumption that George Bush won the election and set in motion a chain of events that were devastating to Al Gore's chances." The other networks quickly followed suit.

Rep. Peter Deutsch (D-Fla.) went further, saying the networks' exit polls were right and that "if the vote had been counted in Florida, Al Gore would be president of the United States." Rep. Bobby Rush (D-Ill.) demanded a hearing on minority voters being "harassed by police across the country."

And when it was his turn, Rep. Steve Buyer (R-Ind.) pronounced it "distasteful" that the witnesses had to wait while the lawmakers, seeing the television cameras, "get excited and pontificate," then briefly pontificated himself.

The gist of the panel members' question was: What was television's great rush to call an excruciatingly close election in the middle of the night?

The network news chiefs, acknowledging that they are driven by competition, said they would continue using exit polls while trying to fix the problems that produced the Nov. 7 fiasco in which they twice had to retract their Florida projections. ABC News President David Westin said the past success of exit polls "led to hubris on our part," while CBS's Heyward said there was a danger of "demonizing" such surveys.

Ailes, a former GOP consultant, said that when approached by exit pollsters Republicans "tend to think it's none of your business, and Democrats want to share their feelings." This leads to "some bias," he said, "unless you send the Republicans to sensitivity training."

The executives, who also included CNN Chairman Tom Johnson and Associated Press President Louis Boccardi, supported legislation to mandate that all national polls close at the same time and promised not to "call" any states before that.

Next time, the network bosses said, they would not use exit polls to call very close races and they would soften their language in projecting likely winners. CNN's Johnson said his network would finance a second source of exit polls.

Waxman asked about what he termed a "rumor" that Jack Welch, chairman of General Electric, NBC's corporate parent, "intervened to call the election for George Bush." He offered no proof.

NBC's Lack called that "untrue," "rather foolish" and "just a dopey rumor," saying Welch was watching the coverage in the newsroom but not calling the shots. Waxman said the panel might subpoena an internal tape of Welch made that night.

Earlier, columnist Ben Wattenberg, co-author of a report for CNN calling its election night coverage a "news disaster," said the networks "were competing with themselves to play beat-the-clock in a way that was ultimately truly senseless."

"Something went very wrong," said Joan Konner, another co-author and former dean of Columbia University's journalism school.

Markey placed the blame on Voter News Service, the exit poll consortium financed by the networks, which has acknowledged providing faulty data. "The news anchors don't have PhDs in statistics," he said. "VNS failed them."

Markey also objected to the hearing's investigative focus, saying there shouldn't be "a criminalization of news-gathering. We should avoid confusing this with the tobacco hearings or the Firestone tire hearings." Tauzin said the panel was following normal fact-finding procedures.

Rep. Sherrod Brown (D-Ohio), invoking Fox's use of Bush cousin Ellis as head of its decision desk, asked whether the networks should have a policy against hiring candidates' relatives. "I think that's preposterous," Wattenberg said.

Brown responded by calling Fox "the most conservative politically of the major networks." Wattenberg shot back that "there are a lot of Americans who think the other networks are too liberal."

In his prepared testimony Ailes defended Ellis, who repeatedly spoke to his cousins George and Jeb Bush on election night. Ailes called Ellis a "consummate professional" who, in using his "family connections," acted as "a good journalist talking to his very high-level sources."

The most curious moment may have come when Tauzin declared: "Americans don't like exit polls. Perhaps they ought to adopt a simple strategy and that's to lie about how they voted."

On June 1, 2001, when all was said and done, all the major networks and the Associated Press decided to retain the Voter News Service, using a new statistical model and updated procedures.

And, as they say, *the rest is history*. (Or is it *news*?)

APPENDIX A

Your First Journalism Job

by Dave Cupp

D ave Cupp is the news director of WVIR-TV in Charlottesville, Virginia. He's been at this television station for many years. Dave has launched many broadcast careers. He lectures students each year at the RTNDA and other conventions. He's created a very informative guide for new journalists:

Make a Good First Impression

- The first two weeks are critical. Any impression, bad or good, made then will last for months.
- Do your homework. Learn your way around town. Read the local paper every day before the morning meeting. Study the archives so you know the background on all the stories being covered every day. Get up to speed fast.
- Do the little things right, and the big ones will take care of themselves.

- Focus on details. You have a thousand to learn. Make someone show you how to do something three times and they'll resent it. Make them show you twice and they'll expect it. Make them show you only once and they'll be impressed.

Make a Commitment to Ethics

- Seek truths...but minimize harm.
- Act independently...but remember stakeholders.

Make a Commitment to Quality

- Become known for it.
- Be the reporter who always gets the details right.
- Be the reporter who always runs the spell checker.

Do Your Own Reality Check

- You've chosen a profession that operates 24/7, 365 days a year.
- As the old saying goes, "The hours are bad, but at least the pay is lousy."
- Recognize that may mean six-day work weeks, early-morning and weekend shifts, working on holidays, and missing family trips because they occur during sweeps. Get over it, accept it and don't make your boss feel like Ebenezer Scrooge for asking you to work on Christmas Day. If you're a newcomer, you should already have volunteered to.

Always Carry the Tripod

- Literally—don't go out the door carrying nothing but a reporter's notebook while your photog is loaded down like a pack mule (assuming this is a non-union shop).

- In a broader sense, always look around you…see what needs to be done…and pitch in to help. Favors you do for your frazzled colleagues will never be forgotten.

Keep Your Boss' Boss off Your Boss' Back

- As a middle manager, your news director lives in a purgatory between the rock of Upper Management Mandates and the hard place of Employee Druthers.
- Cooperate, and he or she won't forget it.
- Choose not to cooperate, and that won't be forgotten either.

Avoid Office Politics

- It is a waster of time and a destroyer of morale.
- Stay above it, and you will earn a surprising amount of respect.

Develop Your Own Style

- Work to eliminate your weakness.
- Cultivate your strength.

Stick Around

- Never stay anywhere less than a year.
- Don't make your news director hire twice for the same job within 12 months.
- By leaving too quickly you are not doing yourself any favors. You'll benefit from the extra seasoning…and your résumé will benefit from the extra stability.

Make a Good Last Impression

- The last two weeks are critical. You'll never have a chance to undo an impression made during them.

- Don't settle scores.
- Don't get short-timer syndrome.
- Work as hard on your last day as you did on your first.
- Give full notice. Two weeks' notice means two weeks of work, not, "Gee, could I take some of my vacation time during my notice period?"
- Deliver your resignation in writing, in person, during business hours. Don't call your boss over the weekend, or while he or she is on vacation, to give notice. If your new employer balks at the extra time, explain the circumstances and your reluctance to treat your boss shabbily. They'll understand, and your new boss will be glad to have an employee concerned about treating the old boss well. If he or she isn't, you don't want to work for them anyway.

APPENDIX B

Responsible Journalism Forum

I asked news executives from across America to comment on what responsible journalism means to them.

Company Presidents, CEOs and General Managers

Reporting the truth is the cornerstone of responsible journalism. In television news, where images are joined to words to tell a story, it is essential to apply the same objective standard to visual information that we would place on the spoken word. If we succeed in doing that, we will enlighten our viewers and improve our society.

David Westin, President, ABC News

People understand that democracy depends on a free press, but just as importantly, real democracy depends on a fair press.

Roger Ailes, Chairman & CEO, FOX News

Responsible journalism seeks to accurately reflect important and interesting information in a timely fashion doing no harm unless the social good achieved out balances the harm.
Jack Fuller, President, Tribune Publishing

Responsible journalism requires our stations to cover the news in an objective manner with our only concern being the interest of our viewers (and listeners) and the interest of our communities at large.
Jeff Smulyan, Chief Executive Officer,
Emmis Communications

Responsible journalism is an oxymoron. Responsible reporting is what we should strive for. Report the events factually and objectively and let the reader/viewer decide. Be a good reporter. When reporters begin to think of themselves as journalists they begin to educate and instruct and this is when responsible reporting goes out the window.
Barry Drake, Broadcast CEO

As a CEO, responsible journalism means: Doing "right" by the communities you serve. "Right" means reporting all the news that affects those that live in your coverage area. The good news and the bad, putting a responsible light on crime that doesn't make it the number one story, but places it as its part in the overall mix of events. Focusing instead on national trends and how those trends play out in the local market and the people in it. Doing tough stories where they are called for on businesses owned by prominent individuals regardless of their position in the community or as advertisers. Most importantly getting all sides to all stories always being careful to point out different opinions that allow viewers to make sensible meanings about the events of the day.
Barry Baker, Managing Director, Boston Ventures

Responsible journalism is one, not to get sued. Two, not to go on a witch hunt for the sake of a story—let's not ruin someone's life by pounding the same material over and over again. Sales does not run the news department. However, I do not see a conflict of interest when the news department does a story and uses a client for an expert opinion.

Marty Ostrow, General Manager, WTAJ-TV, Altoona

If in fact journalism is the first draft of history, it is incumbent on us to seek not only speed and accuracy but perspective as well.

Bob Franklin, General Manager, KNTV, San Jose

News Directors and Managers

What was responsible ten years ago is not responsible today. But, there is one common thread. We are paid in this business to make snap judgments on what goes in our newscasts and special reports. Whenever we have to make these decisions we try to do so in as informed a manner as possible. We should not let the competitive nature of television news dictate what we put on the air.

Jeff Wald, News Director, KTLA-TV, Los Angeles

Responsible journalism is being accurate and fair. Telling both sides of a story without letting your emotion dictate the content of the story.

Anthony Maisel, News Director, KDAF-TV, Dallas

Responsible journalism to me means understanding the impact and power of what we produce every day. Whether it's the written or spoken word or the pictures and sound, our stories affect people. We must be level-headed in our thinking and take our jobs seriously. Many of us entered this profession to make a difference in society. It's our responsibility to make sure we make a positive contribution and not a negative one.

Jonathan Knopf, General Manager/News Director, News 12, New Jersey

Responsible journalism is reflected in a person's state of being, rather than just doing a thorough and fair job on a particular story, but living it as an exemplary citizen of the community.

It's significantly more than flying a helicopter around at 500 feet showing police chasing a burglary suspect.

After all, we're here to make this a better place to live. A better community. A better society.

Peter Nuemann, News Director, WEAR-TV, Pensacola

A responsible journalist seeks the truth, asks the tough questions and reports the results in a fair and balanced manner.

Scott Diener, Vice President of News, KNTV, San Jose

Responsible journalism: attempt to be honest and fair in gathering the news and try to treat individuals with respect and try not to cause harm or distress.

Alan Little, News Director, KABB-TV, San Antonio

Responsible journalism is the journalism of hope...going beyond body bags, fire trucks and cops and going directly to the hearts and minds of our customers and, oh yeah, being memorable, too, in a 300-channel universe.

Bob Yuna, News Director, WKBW-TV, Buffalo

Responsible journalism equips people with facts and context, enabling them to reach more informed opinions and to make better decisions for themselves. That can mean something as mundane as which route to take to work or how to dress the kids for school. It can also involve matters much more profound, such as how to be a better parent, how to vote, or how to engage more effectively as a community member. I'm still a believer in the old SPJ Code of Ethics, which calls on journalists to seek the truth and report it as fully as possible, to minimize harm in reporting, to remain editorially independent in their coverage, and to be accountable for the consequences of their actions.

Scott Liben, News Director, KSTP-TV, Minneapolis

For local television, we are the mirrors of the events that affect the residents of our communities. Our coverage of those events must be fair and balanced. We are also residents of the community and have to live with those we cover.

Jim DePury, News Director, WPMT-TV, Harrisburg

Responsible journalism means going home and feeling good about what you did that day. You didn't cross any lines and you informed the viewer in an interesting, factual and unbiased manner.

Debbie Bush, News Director,
WRTV, Indianapolis

What we do comes with a sense of privilege and responsibility. We are charged with the mission of pursuing the highest obtainable form of the truth each day. But, as broadcasters, we also have a duty to operate in the public interest. It would be easy if we could say that there was one set of rules that always guided how we performed our jobs. But there isn't. Each day we must go through the practice of making good decisions that inform the public and minimize the harm.

Angie Kucharski, News Director,
KCNC-TV, Denver

Responsible journalism: We, as journalists, have tremendous power to inform the public but also to influence public opinion. Though we try to report stories in an impartial manner, journalists are human and we have opinions of our own. That's why it's so important for us to consider the many elements that go into our storytelling. We must consider who is affected by our story. If there's a victim in our story, are we being fair to that person and to that person's family? How will our story impact our audience? And what about our responsibility to our industry? Will the story we tell further spoil the reputation of the media in general? Ours is an industry so many people already love to hate.

Carol Scheer, Executive Producer,
KSTP-TV, Minneapolis

Responsible journalism is having the integrity within yourself to work hard getting the information for the audience so they know the truth about your story.

Nancy Tully, Assistant News Director,
KDNL-TV, Saint Louis

Reporters and Anchors

As a reporter it's my responsibility to gather information for people who cannot themselves be there or see that, or hear that, because they are leading their own busy lives, and bring it to them in a form that is both accurate and intelligible.

Sam Donaldson, ABC News

By definition, a journalist takes it upon himself to inform his fellows about events and machinations in society. Then he must apply some kind of yardstick of responsibility.

Patrick Emory, Anchor

Responsible journalism boils down to fairness and accuracy; making sure you give each party involved in your story a chance to state his or her case, and to get the facts straight to the best of your ability. This also means holding off on a story until those criteria are met.

**Mindy Basara, Anchor/Reporter,
WBAL-TV, Baltimore**

Giving people information in a way that is as truthful and as unbiased as it can possibly be and letting them come to their own conclusions...that's responsible journalism.

**Page Hopkins, Anchor,
Bloomberg Television, New York**

A reporter's constant challenge is to be factual, credible and objective. As a reporter, I must report accurately on the issues of the day that affect the lives of our viewers. It is an awesome responsibility.

**Stan Chambers, Reporter,
KTLA-TV, Los Angeles**

"Responsible journalism" is more than fodder for banter in academia. In practicality, it's what lets you sleep at night.

**Donya Archer, Anchor/Reporter,
WTXF-TV, Philadelphia**

Responsible journalism takes on many forms. At Extra, *our research department checks every single word before anything is broadcast; a reporter should do the exact same thing. In our business your reputation is all you've got.*

Danya Devon, Anchor/Host, *Extra*

Around the Industry

Responsible journalism means reporting that allows the authentic voices of many sides to temper the quest for timeliness and protect the accuracy of the story.

Lillian Dunlap, Instructor, The Poynter Institute

Responsible journalism to me means journalism that is fact-based and, whether straight reporting or analysis, faithful to the readers, viewers and listeners first. It does not mean being "objective" all the time. It does mean trying to get as close to the truth as possible, without harming people unnecessarily. Journalism can be simultaneously responsible and harmful, but if so, the harm caused must be balanced against a higher purpose. The public's "right to know" is not sufficient.

Jonathan Alter, Senior Editor, *Newsweek*

Responsible journalism means always making the extra phone call to get all sides of the story, and treating people the way you'd want to be treated if you found yourself in trouble.

Howard Kurtz, Television Critic,
The Washington Post

Responsible journalism is just what they taught us in that first reporting class: be accurate, be fair, be prepared to stand by your work, and don't be so eager to get a story into print or on the air that you forget any of those things.

Gail Pennington, Television Critic,
The Saint Louis Post-Dispatch

Responsible journalism is never having to say you're sorry.

Mike James, Editor, *News Blues*

APPENDIX C

The Codes of Ethics

Radio-Television News Directors Association

Adopted at RTNDA2000 in Minneapolis, September 14, 2000

Preamble

Professional electronic journalists should operate as trustees of the public, seek the truth, report it fairly and with integrity and independence, and stand accountable for their actions.

Public Trust

Professional electronic journalists should recognize that their first obligation is to the public.

Professional electronic journalists should:
- Understand that any commitment other than service to the public undermines trust and credibility.

- Recognize that service in the public interest creates an obligation to reflect the diversity of the community and guard against oversimplification of issues or events.
- Provide a full range of information to enable the public to make enlightened decisions.
- Fight to ensure that the public's business is conducted in public.

Truth

Professional electronic journalists should pursue truth aggressively and present the news accurately, in context, and as completely as possible.

Professional electronic journalists should:
- Continuously seek the truth.
- Resist distortions that obscure the importance of events.
- Clearly disclose the origin of information and label all material provided by outsiders.

Professional electronic journalists should not:
- Report anything known to be false.
- Manipulate images or sounds in any way that is misleading.
- Plagiarize.
- Present images or sounds that are reenacted without informing the public.

Fairness

Professional electronic journalists should present the news fairly and impartially, placing primary value on significance and relevance.

Professional electronic journalists should:
- Treat all subjects of news coverage with respect and dignity, showing particular compassion to victims of crime or tragedy.

- Exercise special care when children are involved in a story and give children greater privacy protection than adults.
- Seek to understand the diversity of their community and inform the public without bias or stereotype.
- Present a diversity of expressions, opinions, and ideas in context.
- Present analytical reporting based on professional perspective, not personal bias.
- Respect the right to a fair trial.

Integrity

Professional electronic journalists should present the news with integrity and decency, avoiding real or perceived conflicts of interest, and respect the dignity and intelligence of the audience as well as the subjects of news.

Professional electronic journalists should:
- Identify sources whenever possible. Confidential sources should be used only when it is clearly in the public interest to gather or convey important information or when a person providing information might be harmed. Journalists should keep all commitments to protect a confidential source.
- Clearly label opinion and commentary.
- Guard against extended coverage of events or individuals that fails to significantly advance a story, place the event in context, or add to the public knowledge.
- Refrain from contacting participants in violent situations while the situation is in progress.
- Use technological tools with skill and thoughtfulness, avoiding techniques that skew facts, distort reality, or sensationalize events.
- Use surreptitious newsgathering techniques, including hidden cameras or microphones, only if there is no other way to obtain stories of significant public importance and only if the technique is explained to the audience.
- Disseminate the private transmissions of other news organizations only with permission.

Professional electronic journalists should not:
- Pay news sources who have a vested interest in a story.
- Accept gifts, favors, or compensation from those who might seek to influence coverage.
- Engage in activities that may compromise their integrity or independence.

Independence

Professional electronic journalists should defend the independence of all journalists from those seeking influence or control over news content.

Professional electronic journalists should:
- Gather and report news without fear or favor, and vigorously resist undue influence from any outside forces, including advertisers, sources, story subjects, powerful individuals, and special interest groups.
- Resist those who would seek to buy or politically influence news content or who would seek to intimidate those who gather and disseminate the news.
- Determine news content solely through editorial judgment and not as the result of outside influence.
- Resist any self-interest or peer pressure that might erode journalistic duty and service to the public.
- Recognize that sponsorship of the news will not be used in any way to determine, restrict, or manipulate content.
- Refuse to allow the interests of ownership or management to influence news judgment and content inappropriately.
- Defend the rights of the free press for all journalists, recognizing that any professional or government licensing of journalists is a violation of that freedom.

Accountability

Professional electronic journalists should recognize that they are accountable for their actions to the public, the profession, and themselves.

Professional electronic journalists should:

- Actively encourage adherence to these standards by all journalists and their employers.
- Respond to public concerns. Investigate complaints and correct errors promptly and with as much prominence as the original report.
- Explain journalistic processes to the public, especially when practices spark questions or controversy.
- Recognize that professional electronic journalists are duty-bound to conduct themselves ethically.
- Refrain from ordering or encouraging courses of action that would force employees to commit an unethical act.
- Carefully listen to employees who raise ethical objections and create environments in which such objections and discussions are encouraged.
- Seek support for and provide opportunities to train employees in ethical decision-making.

Society of Professional Journalists

© 1995 Society of Professional Journalists. ALL RIGHTS RESERVED

Preamble

Members of the Society of Professional Journalists believe that public enlightenment is the forerunner of justice and the foundation of democracy. The duty of the journalist is to further those ends by seeking truth and providing a fair and comprehensive account of events and issues. Conscientious journalists from all media and specialties strive to serve the public with thoroughness and honesty. Professional integrity is the cornerstone of a journalist's credibility. Members of the Society share a dedication to ethical behavior and adopt this code to declare the Society's principles and standards of practice.

Seek Truth and Report It

Journalists should be honest, fair and courageous in gathering, reporting and interpreting information.

Journalists should:

- Test the accuracy of information from all sources and exercise care to avoid inadvertent error. Deliberate distortion is never permissible.
- Diligently seek out subjects of news stories to give them the opportunity to respond to allegations of wrongdoing.
- Identify sources whenever feasible. The public is entitled to as much information as possible on sources' reliability.
- Always question sources' motives before promising anonymity. Clarify conditions attached to any promise made in exchange for information. Keep promises.
- Make certain that headlines, news teases and promotional material, photos, video, audio, graphics, sound bites and quotations do not misrepresent. They should not oversimplify or highlight incidents out of context.
- Never distort the content of news photos or video. Image enhancement for technical clarity is always permissible. Label montages and photo illustrations.
- Avoid misleading re-enactments or staged news events. If re-enactment is necessary to tell a story, label it.
- Avoid undercover or other surreptitious methods of gathering information except when traditional open methods will not yield information vital to the public. Use of such methods should be explained as part of the story.
- Never plagiarize.
- Tell the story of the diversity and magnitude of the human experience boldly, even when it is unpopular to do so.
- Examine their own cultural values and avoid imposing those values on others.
- Avoid stereotyping by race, gender, age, religion, ethnicity, geography, sexual orientation, disability, physical appearance or social status.
- Support the open exchange of views, even views they find repugnant.
- Give voice to the voiceless; official and unofficial sources of information can be equally valid.
- Distinguish between advocacy and news reporting. Analysis and commentary should be labeled and not misrepresent fact or context.

- Distinguish news from advertising and shun hybrids that blur the lines between the two.
- Recognize a special obligation to ensure that the public's business is conducted in the open and that government records are open to inspection.

Minimize Harm

Ethical journalists treat sources, subjects and colleagues as human beings deserving of respect.

Journalists should:
- Show compassion for those who may be affected adversely by news coverage. Use special sensitivity when dealing with children and inexperienced sources or subjects.
- Be sensitive when seeking or using interviews or photographs of those affected by tragedy or grief.
- Recognize that gathering and reporting information may cause harm or discomfort. Pursuit of the news is not a license for arrogance.
- Recognize that private people have a greater right to control information about themselves than do public officials and others who seek power, influence or attention. Only an overriding public need can justify intrusion into anyone's privacy.
- Show good taste. Avoid pandering to lurid curiosity.
- Be cautious about identifying juvenile suspects or victims of sex crimes.
- Be judicious about naming criminal suspects before the formal filing of charges.
- Balance a criminal suspect's fair trial rights with the public's right to be informed.

Act Independently

Journalists should be free of obligation to any interest other than the public's right to know.

Journalists should:
- Avoid conflicts of interest, real or perceived.
- Remain free of associations and activities that may compromise integrity or damage credibility.
- Refuse gifts, favors, fees, free travel and special treatment, and shun secondary employment, political involvement, public office and service in community organizations if they compromise journalistic integrity.
- Disclose unavoidable conflicts.
- Be vigilant and courageous about holding those with power accountable.
- Deny favored treatment to advertisers and special interests and resist their pressure to influence news coverage.
- Be wary of sources offering information for favors or money; avoid bidding for news.

Be Accountable

Journalists are accountable to their readers, listeners, viewers and each other.

Journalists should:
- Clarify and explain news coverage and invite dialogue with the public over journalistic conduct.
- Encourage the public to voice grievances against the news media.
- Admit mistakes and correct them promptly.
- Expose unethical practices of journalists and the news media.
- Abide by the same high standards to which they hold others.

The Associated Press Managing Editors

Responsibility

The good newspaper is fair, accurate, honest, responsible, independent and decent. Truth is its guiding principle.

It avoids practices that would conflict with the ability to report and present news in a fair, accurate and unbiased manner.

The newspaper should serve as a constructive critic of all segments of society. It should reasonably reflect, in staffing and coverage, its diverse constituencies. It should vigorously expose wrongdoing, duplicity or misuse of power, public or private. Editorially, it should advocate needed reform and innovation in the public interest. News sources should be disclosed unless there is a clear reason not to do so. When it is necessary to protect the confidentiality of a source, the reason should be explained.

The newspaper should uphold the right of free speech and freedom of the press and should respect the individual's right to privacy. The newspaper should fight vigorously for public access to news of government through open meetings and records.

Accuracy

The newspaper should guard against inaccuracies, carelessness, bias or distortion through emphasis, omission or technological manipulation.

It should acknowledge substantive errors and correct them promptly and prominently.

Integrity

The newspaper should strive for impartial treatment of issues and dispassionate handling of controversial subjects. It should provide a forum for the exchange of comment and criticism, especially when such comment is opposed to its editorial positions. Editorials and expressions of personal opinion by reporters and editors should be clearly labeled. Advertising should be differentiated from news.

The newspaper should report the news without regard for its own interests, mindful of the need to disclose potential conflicts. It should not give favored news treatment to advertisers or special-interest groups.

It should report matters regarding itself or its personnel with the same vigor and candor as it would other institutions or individuals. Concern for community, business or personal interests should not cause the newspaper to distort or misrepresent the facts.

The newspaper should deal honestly with readers and newsmakers. It should keep its promises.

The newspaper should not plagiarize words or images.

Independence

The newspaper and its staff should be free of obligations to news sources and newsmakers. Even the appearance of obligation or conflict of interest should be avoided.

Newspapers should accept nothing of value from news sources or others outside the profession. Gifts and free or reduced-rate travel, entertainment, products and lodging should not be accepted. Expenses in connection with news reporting should be paid by the newspaper. Special favors and special treatment for members of the press should be avoided.

Journalists are encouraged to be involved in their communities, to the extent that such activities do not create conflicts of interest.

Involvement in politics, demonstrations and social causes that would cause a conflict of interest, or the appearance of such conflict, should be avoided.

Work by staff members for the people or institutions they cover also should be avoided.

Financial investments by staff members or other outside business interests that could create the impression of a conflict of interest should be avoided.

Stories should not be written or edited primarily for the purpose of winning awards and prizes. Self-serving journalism contests and awards that reflect unfavorably on the newspaper or the profession should be avoided.

Society of Business Editors and Writers

Statement of Purpose: It is not enough that we be incorruptible and act with honest motives. We must conduct all aspects of our lives in a manner that averts even the appearance of conflict of interest or misuse of the power of the press.

A business, financial and economics writer should:
- Recognize the trust, confidence and responsibility placed in him or her by the publication's readers and do nothing to abuse this obligation. To this end, a clear-cut delineation between advertising and editorial matters should be maintained at all times.
- Avoid any practice which might compromise or appear to compromise his objectivity or fairness. He or she should not let any personal investments influence what he or she writes. On some occasions, it may be desirable for him or her to disclose his or her investment positions to a superior.
- Avoid active trading and other short-term profit-seeking opportunities. Active participation in the markets which such activities require is not compatible with the role of the business and financial journalist as disinterested trustee of the public interest.
- Not take advantage in his or her personal investing of any inside information and be sure any relevant information he or she may have is widely disseminated before he buys or sells.
- Make every effort to insure the confidentiality of information held for publication to keep such information from finding its way to those who might use it for gain before it becomes available to the public.
- Accept no gift, special treatment or any other thing of more than token value given in the course of his pro-

fessional activities. In addition, he or she will accept no out-of-town travel paid for by anyone other than his or her employer for the ostensible purpose of covering or backgrounding news. Free-lance writing opportunities and honoraria for speeches should be examined carefully to assure that they are not in fact disguised gratuities. Food and refreshments of ordinary value may be accepted where necessary during the normal course of business.

- Encourage the observance of these minimum standards by all business writers.

Guidelines to Ensure Editorial Integrity of Business News Coverage

- A clear-cut delineation between advertising and editorial matters should be maintained at all times.
- Material produced by an editorial staff or news service should be used only in sections controlled by editorial departments.
- Sections controlled by advertising departments should be distinctly different from news sections in typeface, layout and design.
- Promising a story in exchange for advertising is unethical.
- Publishers, broadcasters and top newsroom editors should establish policies and guidelines to protect the integrity of business news coverage.

APPENDIX D

Suggested Reading and Web Sites

Suggested Reading

Dotson, Bob. *Make it Memorable: Writing and Packaging TV News with Style.* Chicago: Bonus Books, Inc., 2000.

Hane, Paula J. *Super Searchers in the News: The Online Secrets of Journalist and News Researchers.* Medford, N.J.: CyberAge Books, Inc., 2000.

Kalbfeld, Brad. *Associated Press Broadcast News Handbook: Manual of Techniques and Practices.* New York: McGraw-Hill Professional Publishing, 2000.

Koppel, Ted. *Off Camera: Private Thoughts Made Public.* New York: Alfred A. Knopf, Inc., 2000

McCoy, Michelle, with Ann S. Utterback. *Sound and Look Professional on Television and the Internet: How to Improve Your On-Camera Presence.* Chicago: Bonus Books, Inc., 2000.

Seib, Philip. *Going Live: Getting the News Right in a Real-Time, Online World.* Lanham, Md.: Rowman & Littlefield, 2000.

Tuggle, C.A., Forrest Carr and Suzanne Huffman. *Broadcast News Handbook: Writing, Reporting, and Producing*. New York: McGraw-Hill Higher Education, 2001.

Utterback, Ann S. *Broadcast Voice Handbook: How to Polish Your On-Air Delivery*. 3rd ed. Chicago: Bonus Books, Inc., 2000.

Utterback, Ann S. *Broadcaster's Survival Guide: Staying Alive in the Business*. Chicago: Bonus Books, Inc., 1997.

Web Sites to Visit

Responsible Journalism official site: **www.responsiblejournalism.net**

American Civil Liberties Union: **www.aclu.org** *Includes information on how to make Freedom of Information Act requests*

American Journalism Review: **ajr.newslink.org**

Columbia Journalism Review: **www.cjr.org**

Investigative Reporters and Editors: **www.ire.org**

National Press Club: **npc.press.org**

Newcity.com: **www.newcity.com** *Articles for print journalists*

Newspaper Association of America: **www.naa.org**

Pew Center for Civic Journalism: www.pewcenter.org

Power Reporting: **powerreporting.com** *Research tools for journalists*

The Poynter Institute: **www.poynter.org**

Radio-Television News Directors Association: **www.rtnda.org**

Reporters Committee for Freedom of the Press: **www.rcfp.org**

Society of Professional Journalists: **www.spj.org**

Index

About the Author

Photo by Suzy Gorman

Jeff Alan is an Emmy award–winning news director and journalist who has written, reported and anchored newscasts for more than a quarter of a century. He has coached young journalists who today are leaders in the industry, both in front of and behind the cameras.

Jeff is the winner of the Ed King Memorial Golden Quill Award and the award for Best Newscast from the National Academy of Television Journalists. He has been an advocate of journalistic excellence while serving as news director at stations in Missouri, Pennsylvania, Tennessee, West Virginia and Arizona.

Notes

- Call a news station, ask for a tour, papers, etc.
  Give ideas, ask about junior reporting*

*Good
Idea